THE ITTMOOR CHRONICLES

# The
# Coldstone Conflict

# THE ILLMOOR CHRONICLES

# The Coldstone Conflict

## DAVID LEE STONE

Hodder
Children's
Books

A division of Hachette Children's Books

This book is for my agent, Sophie Hicks.
If it wasn't for you, the dream of Illmoor
would never have been realized. Thank you
for making me the author I always hoped
I would become (and for putting up with my
tantrums and increasingly bizarre
sense of humour).

# Selected Dramatis Personae
## (ye cast of characters)

| | | |
|---|---|---|
| Blood, Prince | – | Ruler of Legrash. |
| Diveal, Sorrell | – | A dark sorcerer. |
| Funk, Viceroy | – | Ruler of Beanstalk. |
| Goldeaxe, Gordo | – | A dwarf. |
| Hyburni, Burnie | – | A troglodyte. |
| Lambontroff, Loogie | – | Steward of Phlegm. |
| Moltenoak | – | A hooded man. |
| Muttknuckles, Baron | – | Ruler of Sneeze. |
| Obegarde, Jareth | – | A vampire. |
| Quickstint, Jimmy | – | A thief. |
| Slythi, King | – | Ruler of Ungst. |
| Spatula, Effigy | – | A freedom fighter. |
| Teethgrit, Gape | – | A barbarian. |
| Teethgrit, Groan | – | A barbarian. |
| Theoff, Mr | – | Lambontroff's aide. |
| Thungus, Grid | – | A barbarian. |
| Vanquish | – | A dark god. |
| Vanya, Lady | – | Daughter of Visceral. |
| Visceral, Vortain | – | Earl of Spittle. |
| Wustapha, Diek | – | An enchanted boy. |

# ILLMOOR

GRINSWOOD FOREST

LEGRASH

BEANSTALK

CHUDDERFORD

SNEEZE

RIVER WASHOUT

LITTLE IRKESOME

SHINBONE

SHINBONE
FOREST

CRUST

SHADEWELL

GLEAMING MOUNTAINS

CARAFAT JUNGLES

## DULLITCH

# Prologue

Certain stories only need to be told once: they get handed down, like old clothes, from generation to generation. Some get handed down because they're frightening, or whimsical, or good for a laugh. Others get handed down because they're true.

Everyone knew the story of Charney well – at least, well enough to know that it wasn't one. So when the hooded man wandered into Cambleton Valley, he knew exactly what to expect. The town, which was referred to only in hushed whispers, supported the entire werewolf community of Illmoor . . . and strangers were simply not tolerated. In the latter part of the Tri-Age, an agreement had been reached that, in exchange for food

provided by nearby Spittle, the wolves would never leave their town . . . or, more importantly, the valley that secluded it.

Every so often, a stranger would wander in, and become food or, in some extreme cases, a part of the pack.

The hooded man had absolutely no intention of becoming either.

He looked up. The signpost said: **You Are Trying To Leave Charney**. It certainly made its point, he thought.

A wolf howled in the night. It was joined by several more, and the sound grew into a cruel yet pitiful cry.

Stopping on the road to glance up at the moon, the hooded man quickly became attuned to the shadows moving around him, not by sight . . . but by the barely perceivable sounds they made.

'I am unarmed,' he said. 'Move out of the dark, if you've a will to slay me.'

Three wolves detached themselves from the forest fringe and circled the stranger, growling low and slathering with hunger.

'I've never been bitten by a wolf,' said the hooded man, his voice still calm. 'Is it VERY painful?'

The growls became synchronized as another pair of wolves emerged from the undergrowth and joined the pack.

'Hmm . . . this fight is a little bit one-sided, isn't it?' the hooded man continued, dropping his knapsack and taking a step back. 'Am I to face you one at a time, or all at once? Oh, I see, you're preparing to—'

He was cut off as the first wolf leaped at him, knocking him backwards. The hooded man tripped over his knapsack, and groped for the signpost in order to right himself . . . but the beasts were on him: all five, in fact, ripping at his flesh before he'd even hit the ground.

There was a wild struggle before the body fell limp and the wolves began to fight over it: all joined in the feast.

A few moments passed as the five wolves picked at their prey. Then something extraordinary happened . . .

The wolves began to die. Howling with pain and frustration, the first one scrabbled in the dirt, tongue lolling from the corner of its bloodied maws. As its eyes began to fix on infinity, its body changed back into human form . . . and it died.

The stranger, still lying in the middle of the road, began to laugh: a cold, cruel cackle that echoed through the surrounding hills.

The second wolf staggered forward on shaky legs . . . and collapsed in the dirt. This one didn't revert to its human form, as the other had done, but simply died in the shape nature had gifted it. Two more expired in the same way. Of the entire pack, only the largest beast now remained . . . and even *this* magnificent terror was dying as it transformed.

'You . . .' the dirty, bloodied wretch said, pointing at

the hooded man with a shaking, accusatory finger. 'Murderer!'

The stranger, who'd staggered to his feet and was still bleeding profusely, pulled back his hood to reveal a face so grey that it could have belonged to a gargoyle.

'Ha! Why should I mourn your losses? You made a good *meal* of me!'

The wolf man scrabbled in the dirt, his strength beginning to leave him as the poison kicked in.

'B-bad meat,' he managed, weakly. 'B-b-bad blood.'

The hooded man nodded, his skin re-forming. 'Actually, it's neither.'

'Y-you're a necromancer, a demon, a—'

'Oh no, my friend. It's much more than that: I'm . . . *old*.'

The wolf man, expelling his life's breath, croaked: 'Y-you're a god?'

'Wrong again,' said the stranger. 'Though I've always *wanted* to be.'

He kicked the corpse aside and reached for his knapsack.

'I *have* tasted the flesh of a ghoul, mind . . . and the blood of a vampire. I've never eaten werewolf before, but I'm told you taste . . . wonderful.'

He sighed, and opened his knapsack. Far to the east, another series of howls split the silence of midnight. More wolves would come, and quickly; they would all need to be dealt with. Still, there was time . . .

The hooded man produced a bread roll from the fathomless depths of his knapsack, broke off a piece and parted it. Then he ripped a leg from one of the wolves, put it into the roll and began to chew noisily on it.

'Water,' he muttered longingly, after the second mouthful. 'I always like to have water with a meal: it's good for the digestion.'

He rose to his feet and began to look around for the source of running water that he'd heard since his arrival in Cambleton Valley. Before he reached the forest fringe, however, a voice said:

'Well, that's the first time I've ever seen a human take on a pack o' werewolves and come out smilin'.'

The hooded man glanced up at a large, ugly-looking bird with a patch of mangy feathers and a sickly-looking yellow bill.

'A barrowbird,' he muttered. 'How nice: which god have I upset now?'

The bird cocked its head.

'So you eat werewolves 'n' ghouls, and you drink vampire blood; makes you a rare boy, that does.'

The hooded man's scar of a mouth twisted into a smile. 'Thanks for the compliment,' he muttered. 'But really, I've met your kind before and I don't *need* a travelling companion.'

'You must be . . . pretty much a one-off, in fact.'

'Yes, but—'

'You must be . . . *special*.'

'I am. However—'

'In fact,' chirped the barrowbird, hopping along its branch. 'Unless I'm very much mistaken, you must be Moltenoak.'

The hooded man froze. He hadn't heard that name in a very long time . . . and this barrowbird was pushing its luck.

# Previously, in the Illmoor Chronicles

Burnie, the troglodyte chairman of Dullitch Council and founder of the city's secret army, revealed a terrible truth about the death of Viscount Curfew and the existence of his impersonator, the necromancer Sorrell Diveal. Escaping with his life, Burnie fled Dullitch, and was forced to communicate with the rest of the secret army by ravensage. Inside the palace, famed barbarian Groan Teethgrit was tricked by Diveal into releasing a dark god from its cosmic prison. Possessed by the malevolent soul of Vanquish, Groan turned on his own companions and attacked them in a brutal frenzy. The attack was witnessed by three magically disguised members of the secret army who, fearing imminent danger, fled the scene . . .

# Part One
# The Great Escape

# One

It was evening in Dullitch, and a sudden, terrible storm was assaulting the city. Lightning danced from the sky, followed by cracks of thunder so deafening that the city's doomwardens had taken to their pulpits, and were proclaiming the end of creation.

Up at the palace, a determined multitude of guards, maids and cooking staff were deserting the grounds. This exodus was not the result of the storm, but due to the major explosion that had *preceded* it, ripping through the palace's upper floor and throwing everyone into a blind panic. Rumours of Viscount Curfew's death were already circulating widely.

Yet none of the citizens could possibly guess the true

horror of the scene taking place inside the throne room at that very moment.

There was a gasp, and two enchanted swords clattered on to the stone floor.

Gape Teethgrit looked down at the sword protruding from his stomach, and his ever-present smile contorted into shock.

'G-g-groan,' he spluttered, staring up at the blood-red eyes of the *thing* that had until recently been his only brother. 'What have you . . .'

His voice trailed off . . . and he slumped to the floor. Beside him lay the equally still body of a dwarf. Gordo Goldeaxe, famed mercenary and long-time partner of Groan Teethgrit of Phlegm, stared into the void of infinity, blood still trickling from his lips.

'Excellent, master! Excellent!'

A disfigured face emerged from the shadows of the room, followed by a stooped frame that insinuated itself forward. The figure was wrapped in a black cloak, still clutching at the bloody stump where its right hand had been. Sorrell Diveal, fell sorcerer and a highborn lord of Illmoor, hurried over to kneel before the giant form of Groan Teethgrit.

'Lord Vanquish, god of gods, I bow before thee in supplication. Indeed, I already feel myself becoming more powerful again in your presence. I beg you to grant me—'

'**I grant you nothing.**'

The voice was no more than a whisper, a rasp, but it spoke of an evil so great as to be unimaginable.

Diveal looked up, sharply.

'B-but I granted your desires, master! I gave you freedom!'

'**The barbarian did that.**'

Vanquish closed Groan's mighty fist and looked at it, as if examining a rare treasure.

'**Strong,**' said the god. '**So . . . strong. I need more like him if I am to return to power. People will listen to and obey strength . . . not the whining of a spindly wretch like yourself. Groan and his friends will . . . *broaden* my influence.**'

'B-but you killed his friends, my lord.'

Vanquish turned away from Diveal and crouched over the fallen warriors. Then, running his hands along the mortal wounds that had claimed both lives, he began to speak in a low and arcane voice. There was a sudden pulse of sound, and red light streamed from the barbarian's fingertips, surrounding the corpses and causing them to shake uncontrollably.

'**Servants of the Sword,**' came the deadened voice once more. '**Heal . . . breathe . . . rise in my service.**'

The body of Gordo Goldeaxe twitched, and its eyes flicked open. They were larger than they had been in life, and black of pupil. Beside him, Gape was approaching the same state.

'You now possess the souls of two creatures that failed in my service long ago. This is a second chance for you, my friends . . . rise now . . . and do not fail me again.'

The two warriors brought themselves, slowly and awkwardly, to their feet.

'They will make great soldiers in our army,' Diveal tried again, pulling himself up and forcing a hopeful smile. 'Great soldiers indeed.'

'*Our* army?'

'Your army,' the sorcerer corrected himself. 'I meant to say *your* army, of course.'

Vanquish smiled, and it was revealed that Groan's gleaming teeth had rotted and turned black.

'I seek not soldiers, wretch . . . but lieutenants to command my army.'

'Lieutenants?' Diveal shook his head. 'What lieutenants do you need? You have me! I know I'll be a little preoccupied with the running of Dullitch, but really, I—'

'You are not WORTHY to run Dullitch and your preoccupations mean less than nothing to me . . .'

'But you said . . . you *promised* . . . I fulfilled my task . . .'

'Your task, dustling, is to decide where you want to be buried.'

Vanquish raised Groan's mighty sword and hurled it across the room. The blade spun several times and then stopped, frozen, a mere centimetre from the sorcerer's chest. It clattered on to the stones.

'I am not without power myself, master,' Diveal muttered, quickly casting an enchantment to slow the blood-flow from his wrist. 'P-please reconsider . . . I am your most faithful servant. You asked me to disguise myself as Curfew and, with your help, I did it! You asked me to kidnap and replace the viscount; I obeyed! You told me how you were to be freed; I made it happen! I—'

'**You DARE to challenge me.**' The voice of Vanquish now felt to Diveal like a cold laceration.

'N-no master! Of course not . . . yet I must defend myself if you—'

'**Defend yourself, then.**'

It happened in a split second.

Vanquish released a breathtaking stream of magical energy from outstretched fingertips, lightning tendrils that poured through the air and crashed, ablaze, with an equally powerful stream that flew from the opposite direction.

The two figures circled each other, lightning bleeding into lightning, fire against fire.

Mere shadows in the dazzle, Gape Teethgrit and Gordo Goldeaxe stood, jet eyes blank, awaiting instruction from the voice that had called them back. They longed to meet their master's attacker . . . but the icy strength of the dark god's calm held them back.

There was a sudden blinding surge of light . . . and the fires died away. Vanquish had broken off the assault.

Sorrell Diveal was stepping away from his master, eyes wary, remaining hand outstretched before him.

'Dullitch, master: Dullitch is all I ask . . . it's all I've ever wanted! They wouldn't give it to me! They gave it to Modeset and then Curfew! Don't *you* deny me the city as well . . . I beg of you!'

Vanquish curled his lips into an even darker smile.

**'If you love this city so much, Sorrell, then allow me to make you a permanent part of the palace.'**

He raised one of Groan's great hands, and a jet of flame spewed from it. The flame grew on the air, swirling into a great, tumultuous ball of fire that cannoned towards the sorcerer at great speed.

Diveal leaped back and threw up his hand: a wall of ice materialized along his section of the wall, blocking the fireball but melting away in the process.

'Enough!' Diveal screamed, spit glistening on his withered mouth. 'You're just like *them*, denying me my city . . . my birthright! You're . . . you're . . .'

**'You have little or no concept of what I am. Your magical tricks, impressive though they may be, are only afforded from the power I have already given you.'**

'Not true! I trained as a sorcerer in Shinbone *years* before—'

**'You use dark magic against me . . . yet all dark magic used in this land is mine: I infused the very SOIL with it!**

What will you do when my little *sparks* desert you, maggot?'

Diveal backed into a chair, his eyes darting left and right for some means of escape.

'They'll rise up against you,' he whined. 'The troglodyte that escaped my blade, the vampire and his friends. They'll rise up against you and you'll need someone who can—'

'**I have all the strength I will require**,' said Vanquish, a grim finality edging into his voice. '**Soon, all who have stood against YOU will bow before me . . . along with the pathetic inhabitants of this decrepit city. All will know the wrath of Vanquish . . . as will you.**'

A circle of dark water appeared in the air behind Sorrell Diveal, rippling and shimmering as it took form. Even as the sorcerer moved away from it, the circle became a void . . . a gaping maw.

'**The Dark Doorway invites you, Sorrell. Go and rule for an eternity . . . in Limbo.**'

Vanquish turned to his newly resurrected servants.

'**Throw him in**,' he snarled, and strode from the room, dropping Groan's sword in the process.

Gordo and Gape padded forward, surrounding the sorcerer, who was forced to take a step in the wrong direction.

'Get away from me!' he screamed. 'Get away from me!'

Gape lunged at the sorcerer, his black orb eyes reflecting the terror on Diveal's tortured face. Sorrell

evaded the attempt to snatch him, but tripped over Gordo, who had approached from the opposite direction. Together, driving aside kicking and flailing limbs, they lifted the sorcerer into the air and carried him, screaming, towards the shimmering portal.

'No! No! *Noooooooooo!*'

Diveal was thrown bodily into the inky depths of the swirling pool . . . where his voice was quickly consumed by the bubbling darkness beyond.

Gape and Gordo stared blindly at each other, then turned and padded out of the room in pursuit of their master.

The dark portal began to disintegrate, fading from the room like a shredding mist.

# Two

Vanquish stalked through the palace, walking awkwardly at first, as he became used to Groan's tempered stride. A grim smile parted the barbarian's lips as the dark god made his way through the palace's upper floors.

At length, he paused in a narrow doorway, where a middle-aged man with a long moustache sat hunched over a pile of scrolls.

'**You** . . .' he commanded, pointing a hand that quickly developed elongated fingernails in a gnarly crackle of dark energy. His blood-red eyes blazed defiantly, even in the washy light of the afternoon sun. '**RISE.**'

The man jumped up from his chair and immediately

looked around for a sword. Unfortunately, in doing so he locked eyes with the intruder . . . and felt his will drain away.

'**You are General of the Dullitch Army.**'

'I-I am. We're frantically trying to discover the source of the explo—'

'**Very good. I am now King. You will not defy me.**'

'N-no, Your Majesty. N-never, but Viscount Curfew—'

'**Is no more. You recognize me?**'

The general seemed to break momentarily from his reverie in order to squint at the intruder.

'Y-you are King Teethgrit, ruler of Phlegm.'

'**King Teethgrit, indeed? I am a legend here, on this plane?**'

'What? Oh, er . . . yes, Your Majesty. You are known far and wide for your incredible strength and courage.'

'**Good.**'

'B-but if I may say so, Your Majesty; the people of Dullitch will not—'

'**Then they will be subdued. ALL OF THEM.**'

The general bowed his head, eyes once again locked on the red orbs that fixed him to the spot.

'**You will gather together all *senior* guards present in the palace and bring them to the great courtyard. You will not ask why. You will not explain your actions to anyone. You will simply follow these instructions unswervingly . . . and with purpose.**'

Again, the general bowed his head.

'I will, Your Majesty.'

Vanquish stood aside and watched as the little man dashed from the room and bolted off in the direction of the great hall. Then he moved into the general's office and began carefully inspecting its contents. Evidently, it had once been the home of the palace wizard, as it contained all manner of flasks and bottles, along with rows of books stacked haphazardly on rickety shelving.

Vanquish ran his newly grown talons along the display and selected three very different looking containers. There was a miniature box, an ornately decorated flask with a cork stopper and a squat, circular jar.

Taking the deepest of breaths, Vanquish unclasped the box, lifted its lid and exhaled into it. At first, there was only the rush of expelled air, but then a wispy mist emerged from the dark god's mouth and drifted into the box. Vanquish left the lid open for a time, examining the swirling mist within. Then he closed the lid and replaced the box carefully on the shelf, before turning his attention to the remaining containers.

This time, however, his breath was spent in a different way.

'**Mmmmmmmmmmmmmmmmmmmmmmmmmmmm.**'

The hum was low, a negative wall of sound that rumbled through the palace, causing dust to drift down from the ceilings.

Vanquish abruptly ceased his efforts . . . and waited.

After a few minutes, Gape and Gordo appeared

outside the room, both shuffling towards the doorway like mindless zombies.

'**Expel your souls into these.**' Vanquish gestured at the remaining containers. '**Just open the lids, blank your minds and breathe out . . . you'll find it happens naturally. Tonight, we will begin to hunt down and destroy all those who witnessed my possession of the barbarian . . . and all those who would stand in defiance of my rule.**'

Gape and Gordo said nothing. They simply staggered into the room and began to follow their master's instructions.

'**Goooood.**' Vanquish allowed himself a smile. '**Now I must go. I have two very old . . . *friends* to summon.**'

Dullitch was in the throws of a chaotic uproar.

Thanks to the determined efforts of the secret army, rumours of Curfew's death were spreading like wildfire. In the east of the city, Effigy Spatula, who was still believed to be dead by his friends in the secret army, moved liked a poisoned dart between the houses, banging on carefully selected doors to alert the more vocal citizens that their beloved leader was nothing more than a cowardly impostor. In the west quarters, Nazz, together with Obegarde and Jimmy Quickstint (whose magical disguises had unfortunately worn off), peppered the crowds with accounts of Groan Teethgrit's greedy capture of the throne, being careful to leave out the fact that he had been possessed by a dark god in the process. These revelations, together with a few pointed suggestions that the taxes might be rising, quickly mobilized the people of Dullitch into a seething mass of agitators.

It took less than an hour for two vast crowds to appear on either side of Oval Square, both seemingly astonished to see the other.

'Effigy!' Nazz yelled, his voice filled with emotion. The big ogre was staring over the front rank of heads and pointing at the opposite mob. 'Jimmy, Obegarde, look! It's Effigy: he's alive!'

The vampire squinted at the distant figure, and nodded in amazement. Jimmy Quickstint, on the other hand, wasted no time in catching up with his friend.

'Effigy,' he spluttered, arriving in front of Spatula as the two crowds merged. 'Y-you have to listen. Diveal survived the explosion—'

'Then the time for listening is over, old comrade. Now is the time for action. Together, we have rallied the people! Now we are ready to fight!'

'But we *must* get word to Burnie. The situation has—'

'Burnie already knows about Diveal.'

'But you don't understand!' Jimmy pointed back at the palace, spittle flying from his mouth as he spoke. 'Groan Teethgrit is in there, and he's *joined forces* with Diveal!'

'What? The barbarian king of Phlegm?'

'Yes!' Jimmy nodded. 'And Diveal has put a spell on him or something. I watched Groan strike down his best friend with my own eyes! What are we going to do?'

Effigy signalled to the crowd for silence.

'Groan has joined forces with Diveal?' he asked, his brow furrowed.

'Well, not voluntarily, but . . .'

'Either way, they are *invaders* . . . and they have taken the throne of *our* city. Well, worry not; soon, both Groan and Diveal will be crushed under the banner of the People's Army of Dullitch. We don't tolerate "invaders" in this city, be they necromancers *or* barbarians.'

'OK, but Groan Teethgrit—'

'I know; the man's a legend.' Effigy waved the thief into stunned silence. 'But he's crossed the line, Jimmy. And now both he *and* Diveal must pay the price for their despotism. The people will finally have their say!'

The freedom fighter raised a large cone to his mouth. 'EVERYONE TO THE PALACE. BRING DOWN THE GATES. CHARGE FOR YOUR FREEDOM! CHAAAAAAAARGE!'

Effigy's words ringing in their ears, the crowd rushed, en masse, at the palace gates, which were soon trampled beneath them. Thousands of armed and screaming justice-seekers hurtled toward the palace, and stopped dead . . . as a grim silence fell over them.

Effigy Spatula lowered the cone and gasped at the sight that greeted them.

Two obsidian dragons had swooped from the stormy sky to land – great wings folding up behind them – on the lower battlements of the palace.

Effigy swallowed, as the crowd before him began to gasp.

'What in the name of . . .'

The sky over Dullitch turned black . . . and several streaks of lightning lashed the ground. As a fine rain fell from the sky, the only remaining sound was that of a child crying, far off in the distance.

The crowd didn't move; it was as if they'd been frozen to the spot with fear. Dragons were a rarity in Illmoor, but obsidian dragons of this size were thought to be no more than the stuff of legend.

However, reality reasserted itself in their minds when both creatures looked skyward in order to belch two colossal jets of flame into the air.

There was a scream from the crowd . . . and several citizens fainted. Then, as if coming out of a trance, the people of Dullitch turned . . . and ran.

All except the remaining members of the secret army. Nazz, Obegarde and Jimmy Quickstint were staring in frank astonishment at Effigy Spatula.

The freedom fighter, far from retreating, had marched straight into the courtyard and was once again raising both hands to his lips. He seemed

completely oblivious to his sudden lack of support.

'You really think a bunch of illusionary guff is going to keep you and your new master on the throne of the greatest city in Illmoor?' he screamed. 'It's LAUGHABLE! Come out and face your destiny, you and the sorcerous wretch you now serve!'

The dragons both watched Effigy carefully, but neither moved to attack him. Obegarde glared at Jimmy.

'Didn't you warn him?' the vampire screamed. 'We've got no idea what we're dealing with here!'

'I didn't get a *chance* to tell him,' Jimmy yelled back. 'He was too intent on storming the palace.'

'He's going to get us all killed,' Nazz bellowed, thundering towards the courtyard.

Vanquish had now appeared on the balcony, a red cloak draped over Groan's broad shoulders. Gordo Goldeaxe and Gape Teethgrit had staggered awkwardly to stand either side of him.

'Gordo!' Jimmy whispered to Obegarde. 'We saw him cut down . . . what's going *on* here? Do you think Diveal raised him?'

'And the brother, by the look of him,' Obegarde replied. 'They're both just standing there, like trained zombies!'

'You!' Effigy screamed again, raising his voice to an even greater level. 'Come down here and face the PEOPLE!'

Up on the balcony, the shadow extended its arms.

'**Interesting**,' the dark voice boomed. The red eyes closed for a moment, as if in concentrated thought. '**And you are Effigy Spatula . . . freedom fighter. How amusing. Yet your friends don't seem to share your confidence. They cower behind you . . . the grave-digging thief, even the ogre and the vampire . . . whose names will come to me in just a moment. Ah yes – we have Obegarde . . . Jimmy Quickstint and Nazz. YOU THREE WOULD DO WELL TO TURN AND WALK AWAY FROM THIS INSOLENT WRETCH, BEFORE YOU JOIN HIM IN MY DISPLEASURE.**'

Effigy peered up at the great form, but he didn't flinch.

'So you come to rely on the minor magic of a cowardly impostor? Am I supposed to turn and flee at the mere mention of a few names? Ha! Your efforts to deter us from our cause are laughable. We speak as one! You, Groan Teethgrit, are nothing more than a savage: step down from the balcony, and bring your tainted master with you!'

'**I have no master, fool. I am Vanquish; hear me roar.**'

A network of lightning stretched from the sky. Vanquish threw up a hand . . . and absorbed it.

Effigy grinned at the display.

'More illusions!' he cried, as Nazz arrived, panting, beside him. 'What's next, I wonder? A rabbit out of a hat? Vanquish, indeed! The people will—'

'**The people of Dullitch will do nothing, for they will encounter nothing that troubles them. They will see what I want them to see, hear what I want them to hear . . . and forget whatever I wish them to forget.**'

'What, like two dragons? Ha! I've never heard such nons—'

Vanquish held aloft a gloved hand, and then brought it down in a sweeping motion. The dragons fell like two stones dropped down a well, unfurling their wings at the last second and swooping low over the cobbles. Rising aloft once more, they breathed a combined shower of flame at the space where Effigy *had* been standing.

But the freedom fighter was gone, struggling in Nazz's mighty arms as the small group retreated into the shadowy streets of Dullitch.

Vanquish turned to his undead assistants.

'**Go now,**' he growled. '**Kill *all* of these fools . . . along with anyone who gets in your way. The dragons will assist you . . . as will I.**'

# Three

'That was fire!' Effigy screamed, as the group thundered around Oval Square. 'Actual, real, genuine, burning flames! I felt the heat on my face.'

'That's because it wasn't an illusion,' Obegarde yelled. 'The dragons were REAL . . . and Groan Teethgrit has become something . . . terrible.'

'You think so?'

'We all do! He's become Vanquish.'

'Yes! That's the name he used . . .'

The group ran on, Effigy still struggling to free himself from Nazz's grip. 'But who, or what, *is* Vanquish?'

'Somebody who commands dragons,' Jimmy panted.

'We probably don't *need* to know any more than that.'

'Vanquish is a god,' Nazz managed, lowering the freedom fighter on to his feet as he continued to pound the cobbles. 'My people in the hills used to speak of him, on cold winter nights. He's very old; possibly as old as Illmoor itself. The good news is that, as I recall from the legends, at that point he took the form of an immense, multi-tentacled mutation. So let's look on the bright side here: at least he's not totally manifest at the moment!'

'*That* is the bright side?' Obegarde panted. 'Terrific. Absolutely terrific.'

'Can today actually get any worse?' Jimmy screamed. 'We've got two dragons after us, possibly controlled by a dark god, both Groan's companions have been turned into demon zombies *and* there's an impostor sitting on the throne.'

'Doubt that,' said Nazz, mockingly. 'If what *I've* heard about Vanquish is true, it's probably already *eaten* him.'

'Where can we go?' Effigy blurted. 'The sewers?'

Jimmy shook his head.

'No. The sewers in Illmoor are all linked to the streets: we can't use them to get *out* of the city.'

'Where, then?'

'I don't know!'

The group ran on, particularly aware of the shadows rising in the skies behind them.

\* \* \*

Vanquish returned to the throne room, his new face set in a grim smile. Concentrating hard, he raised one hand and snapped his fingers: a ball of energy formed on the air, twisting and turning until it shaped itself into a cone of light.

The dark god took a breath. Then he spoke into it:

'**People of Dullitch, hear me now. Your ears do not deceive you: I speak directly into every mind within the city walls. CLEAR THE STREETS: YOU WILL ALL RETURN TO YOUR HOMES AND AWAIT MY INSTRUCTIONS. DO NOT STRUGGLE, FOR TO DO SO AGAINST MY MIGHT IS FUTILE.**'

Vanquish smiled. Of course, he wouldn't get *all* of them to obey, not immediately . . . but the weak and feeble-minded would bend to his will like thin-stemmed florets in the wind.

The dragons swooped and soared over the empty streets of Dullitch, belching flames at every quarter in order to underline the threat. Far below, Gape and Gordo stalked the streets around the palace, kicking down doors and hunting through any houses that looked like convenient hiding places. The inhabitants of these unlucky dwellings sat, mesmerized – entire families of the chosen possessed, awaiting new orders from the voice that had so terrified their souls . . .

Soon, the streets of Dullitch were deserted and the city was gripped in an icy fist of terror.

The secret army had sensibly decided to split up in an effort to leave the city undetected. Nazz and Effigy had gone west, choosing to negotiate the tree-lined walks of Sack Avenue instead of heading directly for the North Gate. Jimmy and Obegarde had moved in the opposite direction, picking their way towards the Rotting Ferret and, ultimately, the Market Gate.

Unfortunately, they found that route barred.

'It's one of the dragons!' Obegarde whispered, peering from the mouth of an alley that ran alongside Finlayzzon's. 'It's landed on the gate tower: we can't get out!'

Jimmy rubbed his chin with a trembling hand. 'Do you think the other one's on the North Gate?'

'Of course it is! Gods damn it! They've closed us in . . .'

'Where do you think that zombified duo are?'

'Who knows?' Obegarde shrugged. 'They could be *anywhere*. We need to move.'

'But where?'

'The harbour: it's our only choice. Even if they *are* blocking the gates, we might still be able to get out on a ship.'

Jimmy looked doubtful. 'You reckon?'

'What other options are there?'

'None.'

'Exactly. Mind you, I'm not sure quite how we're going to get out of this alley. That dragon can probably spot a cockroach from half a mile away . . .'

Jimmy grinned.

'Leave that to me,' he said and, jumping to his feet, began to sidle carefully along the alley.

'Psst . . . Oi!'

The thief glanced over his shoulder. 'What?'

'Where are you going?'

'Through the door over there!' Jimmy pointed at a small wooden portal which opened on to the alley.

'Why, where does it go?'

'To number thirteen, Market Street.'

'And?'

The thief rolled his eyes. 'And the window in the top back room of thirteen, Market Street can get us on to the roof walkway to number nine. When we get to number nine, there is a beam connecting the roof with the roof of the big green house on The Goodwalk. Then we go along the city wall, over Crest Hill and straight into the harbour.'

Obegarde was silent for a moment. Then he said: 'I've just realized how glad I am that I didn't go with Nazz or Effigy.'

Jimmy winked back at him.

'They don't call me Quickstint for nothing,' he said.

On the other side of town, Effigy Spatula and Nazz were looking out from beneath a battered-up carriage on the south end of Tanner Street. Neither of them had spoken in quite some time, and it wasn't because they had nothing to say to each other. They weren't speaking because the situation in the street had them both holding their breath and praying for a miracle.

One of the obsidian dragons had landed atop the North Gate, and was carefully scrutinizing the street . . . in particular a young girl who was standing, frozen to the spot with fear, in the middle of it.

Nobody moved.

'It's seen her! We've got to *do* something, Effigy; we can't just leave her there to die! She looks about twelve!'

'Stay where you are,' Effigy snapped. 'Don't be a fool.'

'But she's not moving!'

'Neither is the dragon.'

'Yeah, but—'

'Shhh!'

The girl was of medium height, with a pale, pretty face and curly brown hair. Her black robes betrayed her as a pupil of Candleford's new preparatory school for girls.

Effigy squinted up at the dragon; the great beast was beginning to unfurl its wings.

'Effigy!'

'I see it, I see it! '

'What're we going to do? It's taking off.'

'Just stay put, damn it!'

'No!'

Nazz swung out from beneath the carriage and bolted towards the girl, just as the dragon took off from its gate-perch.

'Nazz! Come baaaaack!'

The ogre was oblivious of Effigy's cries; he dashed over to the girl, scooped her into his arms and bolted for the sanctuary of a nearby alley. Effigy could see that he wasn't going to make it: the dragon had already taken flight and was about to dive.

'Arrrgghghghghghghhhhh!' Effigy screamed, rolling out from under the carriage and leaping to his feet. 'IT'S ME YOUR MASTERS WANT, YOU GREAT NOTHING! MEEEEEEEEEE!'

The freedom fighter turned on his heel and ran, the black shadow rising over him with remarkable speed.

He tried to run in an unpredictable zigzag, reasoning that the beast wouldn't be able to use its molten breath if it couldn't focus on a target. He was wrong.

A jet of flame erupted just behind and to the left of him. There were screams as the upper floors of several buildings caught alight. Effigy ran on, but he knew he was done for; the flames had been so close . . . and he couldn't keep up his current pace for long.

'OOOOOOOOOIIIIIIIIII! DRAGON FILTH! TAKE MEEE!'

The booming roar had come from Nazz, who'd appeared at the mouth of the alley, and was waving a heavy-looking length of timber. He swung the wood over

his shoulder, then turned and made straight for the North Gate. The dragon soared and turned on the air; unfortunately for Nazz, it was upon him before he got halfway towards the gate tower.

Effigy, holding back both tears and anger, made a determined effort not to watch the confrontation; instead, he made for the alley Nazz had emerged from . . . and found the girl cowering behind a stack of dustbins.

'On your feet! Quick!'

The girl peered up through streaming eyes. 'He saved me!' she said, in what Effigy couldn't help recognizing was a remarkably well-spoken voice. 'He saved my life and now he's going to die!'

Effigy grabbed the girl by the hand and dragged her to her feet.

'Yes, and if you don't keep up with me now, it will all have been for nothing. What's your name?'

'Vanya.'

'Right, Vanya; I'm Effigy Spatula. C'mon!'

The girl rushed along beside him. Soon they emerged on to Laker Street, where Effigy quickly snatched hold of Vanya's arm and dragged her in the direction of the palace.

'Where do you live?'

'I— my family are from Spittle.'

'Well? Where do you live when you're *here*?'

The girl shook her head and tried to get her bearings.

'At a boarding house on Stainer Street,' she said. 'B-but I've finished for the term; I need to get to my father's ship!'

Effigy almost breathed a sigh of relief. 'Perfect!' he managed. 'Maybe I can leave with you. Now stay close to the walls. If that dragon catches up with us, we're both finished.'

Back at the gate, Nazz staggered. He'd put up a valiant fight, but he was no match for an obsidian dragon. The beast had been toying with him, striking terrible wounds with claws and teeth, but not using its fiery exhalations.

The dragon struck out again, ripping a terrible gash in the ogre's stomach. Nazz faltered, and dropped the timber he'd been carrying. His strength was deserting him. If he could just manage one final burst of speed . . .

Sensing the deterioration of its prey, the dragon spread its mighty wings and landed in the street, folding the great leathery appendages behind it. Then, it reached back and bellowed forth a red-hot spew of flame.

But Nazz had gone.

The ogre ran faster than he'd ever run before, the dragon flapping fiercely behind him. He led the beast a merry dance: over the junction with North Gate, through into the top end of Tanner Street, along Royal Road and down into Palace Street, where he quickly ducked into the Church of the Wormridden.

An acolyte, who would usually have homed in on potential worshipers like a torpedo, watched him with an eerie detachment.

'How do I get out of this place?' the ogre boomed, shoving the acolyte against the wall, hard. 'What's wrong with you? Speak! I need help: how do I get out—'

The largest stained-glass window in the entire city imploded under the immense bulk of the dragon, showering glass shards in every direction.

The great beast crashed on to the pews, which seemed to turn into so many fragile dominoes.

Nazz spun round and hurtled back towards the great double doors, but he hadn't got halfway down the aisle when they too crashed to the ground, revealing the second dragon.

Nazz cursed under his breath; it must have spied its sibling across the city and decided to assist the hunt. Oh, well . . .

The ogre leaped up on to the back of a remaining pew and dashed along it, diving for the far aisle when two colossal jets of flame spewed towards him.

Nazz half crashed, half rolled on to the stone floor, the heat streams pouring into a fireball above him. Struggling to his feet, he managed to reach the font in three strides and, wrenching the great stone basin from its mount, hurled it at the nearer of the two beasts. It bounced off the creature's armoured scales and hit the floor. The dragons advanced.

Nearing exasperation, Nazz turned and made to run again, but this time he tripped and crashed on to the flagstones. He tried several times to get up, but was so tired that he could actually feel his strength ebbing away . . .

The dragon he'd hit with the font suddenly moved – incredibly fast for its size. Craning down, it belched forth a jet of flame that lit up the entire sanctuary.

Nazz the ogre managed one last, terrible scream as the fires of hell consumed him.

# Four

Jimmy and Obegarde stopped dead in their tracks. They had reached the top of the Tor, which gave them a magnificent view over the harbour.

'It's them,' Obegarde said. 'Both of them: they're guarding the harbour, one at each end.' He turned to Jimmy with a resigned look on his face. 'That's every exit covered; Vanquish must be controlling them.'

Jimmy sniffed, looked down at his shoes.

'We're stuffed, then,' he muttered. 'We either hand ourselves in to a dark god, get incinerated by dragonfire, or take on two of the possessed who were legendary warriors *before* they became undead.'

The vampire sighed. 'I wonder how far Effigy and Nazz got . . .'

'I don't even want to think about it,' said Jimmy, sadly. 'But we have to get a message to Burnie, somehow – and that means at least *one* of us getting out on a ship. Preferably Effigy; he's the only one who actually *knows* where Burnie is!'

'You really think the troglodyte will be able to do something?'

Jimmy shrugged. 'No, but he's a damn sight smarter than we are – no offence.'

'Then there's only one thing for it.' Obegarde took a deep breath, then shook off his cloak. 'You go; I have to fight them.'

'What?' Jimmy boggled at him. 'Are you out of your bloody mind? They'll carve you up!'

'It's a diversion! Besides, I'm undead: they'll have to decapitate me or at the very least stake me. Either way, I'll last a damn sight longer than you!'

'But it's suicide!'

'So is waiting here to be caught and killed! I'll go for the pair of them, and you go for the ship.'

'But it's—'

'Deal?'

'But—'

'DEAL?'

'All right, damn it! All right.'

Obegarde concentrated hard, his nails and teeth

elongating as he prepared to move for the harbour. When he finally did shift, it was with such speed that Jimmy, who'd been standing right beside him, could make out nothing more than a blur.

He watched as the shimmering form flickered along Royal Market, flashed past the treasury and crashed, with surprising force, into the creature that *had* been Gape Teethgrit. At the opposite end of the harbour, Gordo Goldeaxe turned, like a puppet on a string, and staggered over to join the combat.

Jimmy wasted no time; he sprinted down Crest Hill, negotiated the south side of Royal Market Place, leaped three barriers blockading the harbour . . . and did a double-take. Effigy Spatula had appeared at the far end of the docks, a young girl trailing after him. They were heading for the quay.

Jimmy felt a sudden surge of despondency: Nazz was nowhere to be seen. Could the great ogre really have fallen? It didn't bear thinking about.

He returned his attention to the harbour, where Obegarde was struggling with the two possessed warriors.

Jimmy gritted his teeth and rolled up his sleeves: he couldn't just leave the vampire to his fate. They'd been through too much together . . .

Obegarde spun in the air, slashing at Gordo with his fingernails. The strike cut a line across the dwarf's armour, but couldn't penetrate any further. In reply to the attack, Gordo brought up his battleaxe in a wild sweep. The vampire managed to evade the move, but in doing so he fell straight into the arms of Gape. The big barbarian lifted Obegarde over his head and threw him into a stack of barrels.

There were a few seconds of silence before the vampire exploded out of the stack like a cannonball. This time, he leaped through the air, aiming a kick that caught Gape squarely in the chest and sent him crashing to the ground.

Landing awkwardly, Obegarde managed to duck down and sweep the dwarf's legs out from under him. Gordo grasped at thin air, but went down, hard.

Obegarde was already back on his feet; delivering a mighty blow to Gape's chin which resulted in a sickening thud, he then wrenched the moaning barbarian on to his knees and began to pummel the living daylights out of him.

Gape quickly put a stop to the attack by driving his cannonball head into Obegarde's stomach. The vampire doubled up, allowing Gape to produce a sword from his belt and drive the pommel into Obegarde's face.

The vampire went down, but managed to roll aside before the barbarian could follow up the strike.

Gape drew a second sword and advanced on his foe, giving Gordo time to recover from his fall.

Obegarde watched the approaching barbarian with

mounting unease, narrowly evading the first lunge and ducking to avoid the second. Instead of waiting for a third sweep, he threw a punch that, fortunately for him, caught Gape's upper arm. Seizing the initiative, he leaped in the air and kicked the first sword out of the warrior's grip, watching it as it flew past him.

Obegarde grinned, quickly sidestepping as he noticed the dwarf rising to his feet.

'Looks like we're even, white-eyes,' he snapped. 'Now are you and your soul-sharing friend going to play nicely, or am I going to have to kill you both?' He backed away again, glancing down at the strange engravings on the sword hilt.

'Hmm . . . looks like this one's enchanted,' he muttered, circling the duo. 'A pity the true wielder isn't around to command it, eh?'

Gape Teethgrit's white eyes showed no sign of recognition.

*Gods,* Obegarde reflected, *he really isn't in there, is he?*

Sensing the vampire's pause for thought, Gape rushed forward, driving his blade out in front of him in a desperate lunge. Obegarde stepped aside, parrying the drive with comparative ease. A second thought caused him to turn again, just in time to knock aside the dwarf's first spirited attempt to decapitate him with the battleaxe.

Obegarde danced through the melee, blocking left, dodging right, until he stood, once again, facing down both the warriors. Until today, he'd never fought with a sword, but supernatural ability to read minds was giving him an edge . . . especially when the minds in question had thoughts as slow and predictable as this.

He shook himself from his reverie; Gape and Gordo were moving in for a second round of attacks.

Obegarde took a few steps back, and walked right into Jimmy Quickstint.

Across the harbour, Effigy and Vanya were approaching the West Quay.

'Which one is your father's?' Effigy demanded, deliberately turning the girl away from the conflict in order to focus her attention on the ten or twelve ships lined against the quay.

'It's called the *Royal Consort*; father usually has it waiting right at the very end of the quay.'

Effigy rushed the girl along.

'Is *that* it?' he said, gasping at the sheer magnificence of the square-rigger that dominated the last *three* mooring bays. 'Who on Illmoor is your father; a lord of some sort?'

'No – actually, he's an earl.'

'But there's only one earl in Illm—' Effigy looked sharply at the girl. 'You're Lord Visceral's daughter?'

'Yes.'

'And you go to school *here*?'

'Of course: I *am* thirteen years old, and Candleford is

already thought to be the best preparatory school in Illmoor.'

'Ha! Not when it's been reduced to a great pile of ash! Quickly!'

They hurried up the long-plank that had been stationed to bridge the gap between dock and ship – but the way was quickly barred by a sturdy-looking rogue with gold teeth.

'Aye up, little miss,' he said, his grin a blinding gleam. 'An' who's this 'un?'

'This is Effigy Spatula, Captain. He and his friend have just saved me from almost certain death, and there are dragons behind us, so *please* just—'

'Dragons? Tom! Tom! I told you that was a dragon I saw go over earlier! That's ten crowns you owe me!'

A second crewman appeared at the entrance to one of the cabins.

'Well, I'll be damned!' he said.

'Can we *please* get going,' Vanya demanded. 'It's imperative that my father knows what's going on here!'

'I'll second that,' Effigy agreed, surprised and a little annoyed that a girl so young knew words like 'imperative'.

Several more crewmen appeared and, under orders from the captain, began to release the ship from its moorings.

\* \* \*

'What are you doing here?' Obegarde screamed at Jimmy, as the warrior-zombies approached. 'I told you to go for the ship!'

Jimmy gritted his teeth, brandishing a crowbar he'd found wedged inside a barrel-top. 'I'm not leaving you behind, Obegarde. Either we both go . . . or we stay.'

The vampire didn't have time to reply before Gape lunged at him with yet another wide strike. Jimmy leaped atop a barrel and managed, much to his own astonishment, to somersault backwards over Gordo, landing behind him.

He swung the crowbar with all his might, catching the dwarf across the back of his head and sending him crashing to the floor.

Obegarde parried another attack from Gape, cutting the barbarian a vicious slash across the chest as he faltered.

'Get out! Just go! I can't watch out for you *and* defend myself *and*—'

He glanced over at Jimmy, who was standing next to the prone figure of Gordo Goldeaxe and looking very pleased with himself.

'Jimmy . . .' Obegarde started, his face a mask of horror. 'What are you doing? Effigy is going for a ship: follow *him*!'

'What? No way! Look, I've dealt with this one pretty well, wouldn't you s—'

'No!' Obegarde screamed. 'Behind you!'

Jimmy Quickstint spun around, just in time to see the two dragons drop from the sky and dive towards him.

The thief's legs were a blur: he moved so fast that, for a moment, Obegarde was given to wonder if the gods were assisting him. The dragons converged on the spot he'd occupied seconds before, one narrowly avoiding the other as they came to ground.

Obegarde gasped, but he didn't have time to fall back before Gape lunged at him once more.

Jimmy wasn't hanging around: his escape dash had turned into a determined run for the quay.

Obegarde summoned all his concentration, then jumped on to Gape's back and transformed into a snake. Gape screamed as the reptile curled around his neck and chest, constricting flesh and bone. The barbarian blundered around, flailing madly with his free arm, scratching and biting the snake as his strength faded. Eventually, he managed to wriggle free of the serpent's grip. Snatching hold of its tail, he flung it into the air and snatched up his sword in order to slice it in two. Obegarde, however, was changing form again. The resulting bat flapped over Gape's sword arm and rose into the air with remarkable speed. The barbarian tried, rather pointlessly, to give chase, but tripped and collided with a stack of barrels.

Now, rain was pelting the harbour in torrents.

The dragons had mysteriously ceased their pursuit of

Jimmy Quickstint. They both hung in the air as if hooked on giant, invisible hangers.

Obegarde flew after the thief, who was now a fast-accelerating speck on the quayside.

Gordo, meanwhile, had regained consciousness and scrambled on to his stubby feet. The dwarf managed to regain tight hold of his battleaxe. Turning his head to the sky, he swung it at the dragons in a gesture of defiance.

'Get after them!' screamed the possessed voice. 'Get after them, or face the master's wrath.'

The dragons turned in the air and, flapping noisily, headed back toward the city gates.


'Effigy! Effigy!'

The ship, finally released from the docks, began to drift . . . but not before a lone figure had leaped from the quay and caught hold of the rope ladder several crewmen were attempting to haul up.

'Oi!' screamed the golden-toothed pirate. 'Get the hell off my shi—'

'It's OK, it's OK!' Effigy spluttered, staying the man's arm. 'He's with me.'

'AND?'

'And you can let him aboard, thank you, Captain,' Vanya finished, smiling sweetly. 'Dullitch has become an extremely dangerous place, and a few extra passengers will not noticeably slow our progress.'

The captain nodded, but somewhat reluctantly.

'Right you are, little miss,' he growled, eyeing the dishevelled, breathless figure with nothing less than total disdain.

'O-o-obegarde's fighting the . . .'

'I guessed.' Effigy hung his head. 'He and Nazz have saved us both. May the gods spare them pain.'

As the ship moved slowly out of the harbour, Effigy turned and slumped on to a nearby barrel.

'Jimmy Quickstint, I'd like you to meet Vanya Visceral, daughter of the Earl of Spittle. She's going to help us, if she can.'

Jimmy nodded at the girl briefly, then put his head in his hands and moaned.

'It's been a rough day,' Effigy explained. 'And we've lost two very good friends.'

'I understand,' Vanya said, turning sympathetic eyes away from Jimmy. 'I totally underst– who's that?'

As Effigy and Jimmy both turned, the girl pointed to the upper deck . . . where a vampire had landed, upside down, in the rigging.

Obegarde unhooked his foot and crashed to the deck, rolling sideways to avoid several sword-strikes from the alarmed crew.

'Easy! Easy!' he yelled, jumping to his feet. 'Give me a break, here . . . I've just fought a pair of zombies and two ruddy great dragons – can I have a few minutes' break?'

'Leave him alone!' Jimmy shouted, his face flushed with relief. 'That's our friend!'

The captain turned to Vanya.

'I appreciate your charitable nature, miss, but how many strays are we expected to take on board, here? This one's a flamin' gravewalker!'

'Only on my mother's side,' Obegarde added, avoiding the swords and staggering towards the group. 'But I'm really quite harmless, unless I get peckish. Call me Obegarde.'

'Um . . . hello,' said Vanya, nervously.

Jimmy's face was all smiles.

'You're amazing!' he said. 'Absolutely amazing.'

'That's me.'

'One thing I've always wondered, though: what happens with the clothes . . . ?'

'It's a concentration thing,' Obegarde informed him, with a smirk. 'If your mind wanders, so do your trousers.'

Effigy smiled at the conversation, but quickly moved to change the subject. 'Vanya, your father is on the High Council of Illmoor, isn't he?'

The girl nodded, causing Obegarde to make a face at Jimmy, who quickly mouthed the word 'Visceral' to him.

'Yes. He has a special seat on the permanent council, along with Viscount Curfew and Prince Blood,' said Vanya.

'Viscount Curfew is dead.'

'D-dead? No he isn't! I mean, how? When?'

'It's a long story, but the High Council needs to know that a dark god has been unleashed upon Dullitch. If

something isn't done soon, all the citizens will die . . . and there will be more than dragons hunting the streets . . .'

Gordo helped the dazed Gape to his feet, then lowered his axe and went into a sort of voluntary trance.

There was a noise like a miniature thunderclap, and a fiery image of Groan appeared, hovering on the air and making the raindrops sizzle.

'**The ogre has been eliminated**,' said the voice within. '**My pets made short work of him, yet I detect that you do not have news of equal success . . .**'

Gordo bowed. 'Indeed, master,' he said solemnly, his voice echoing with ethereal resonance. 'The vampire and his friend have *temporarily* eluded us . . .'

'**Do not think you bring me news, servant. My pool of second sight shows me all of Dullitch, and I observe everything within it. Enemies within these walls have no way of hiding from me . . .**'

'Indeed, master . . .'

'**Strange then, that I cannot sense the freedom fighter at all . . . can that be yet another of your mistakes?**'

'No, master. He could not have sneaked past us.'

'**The others did.**'

'Yes master, but, begging your mercy, the dragons chose not to pursue the two rebels that . . . escaped.'

The image of Groan flickered slightly.

'**That is because dragons, unlike yourselves, are**

thinking creatures: they are aware that my power to support them is earthed firmly in this continent. The oceans have their own gods . . . who grant me no dominion. Your ineptitude has cost me two – possibly three – souls . . .'

Gordo's empty eyes dimmed.

'Master.'

'. . . **souls who will sneak back on to this continent and bring me nothing but trouble wherever and however they can. You have failed me. Both of you.**'

'We beg your mercy, master.'

'**Beg not, for I have none. Return to me** . . . **and pray that you find Spatula on your way.**'

Gordo bowed, and the image vanished.

Effigy marched up and down the deck, muttering to himself and occasionally stamping his feet. Obegarde, exhausted, had curled up on a makeshift hammock between two half-masts and gone to sleep.

'Can't this damn ship go any faster?' Jimmy yelled, watching the harbour with keen eyes.

'Not unless the wind picks up,' said the captain, evenly. 'There's no magic wand that drives this vessel . . .'

Effigy cast a sidelong glance at the thief. 'You think the earl will believe us?'

'Of course he will,' said Vanya, calmly. The young aristocrat emerged from the cabin with an urn and

several oddly-shaped cups. 'My father is a very trusting man.'

'Not from what I've heard,' Jimmy muttered, suddenly smiling weakly when he saw that the girl was glaring at him.

'Well you've heard *wrong* then, haven't you? Spittalian tea, anyone?'

Effigy looked at the girl in mock amazement.

'You know, considering your age and everything you've witnessed today, I must say you're managing to remain incredibly calm . . .'

Vanya smiled, and turned back to the captain.

'Could you fetch a ravensage from the cabin? I need to send an urgent message ahead.'

'W-wait!' Effigy hurried over to the girl, his eyes alight with excitement. 'You have a ravensage, here on board?'

Vanya nodded.

'Yes, indeed. We have three, in fact. Did you want to send a message?'

Jimmy and Effigy shared a glance.

'Yes, we do,' they both said, in unison.

Vanquish sat on the throne of Dullitch, his red eyes gleaming in the shadowy dark. His mind was picking its way through the streets of the city, carefully searching every house, every alleyway for *outlines*. If his new servants couldn't find Effigy Spatula, there was absolutely no doubt that *he* could . . .

His vision crept onward, through Royal Road, Market Place, Oval Square, Tanner Street, through The Goodwalk, Stainer Street, Burrow Street, Sack Avenue. Infuriating . . . there was no sign of him . . . not even the merest possibility of an outline . . . except . . . there, *there* at the harbour . . . was the memory of all three. So Spatula *had* slipped past them . . .

Vanquish let out a cry of anger, and slammed his fist on to the arm of the throne.

They would pay for their mistake; both of them would pay . . . *dearly.*

# *Five*

Ravensage were a species of bird set apart by their innate ability to locate even the most obscure of specified destinations. Once, long ago, they had been ordinary ravens. However, in common with the calling-crows of Rintintetly and the barrowbirds of Grinswood, they had, at some undisclosed point in the past, had a serious run-in with the magical arts.

These days, they were largely taken for granted. Still, a bird that could take a random description like 'the place where three Y-shaped trees meet at a crossroads' and actually *find* the site was a bird worth existing.

The raven flew high over the Nasbeck Ocean. For a

time it headed south, towards the distant land of Trod, but a sudden change of direction saw it fly west and, ultimately, north. At length, the ocean gave way to dry land. In its turn, the land became jungle.

Carafat sprawled in every direction, home to more dangerous species than Grinswood and Rintintetly combined. It was rumoured that a vast city existed far beneath the jungle. Then again, in Illmoor, there were rumours about *everything*.

The raven glided for a time, turning west again before coming to land on a rocky outcrop on the edge of the trees. It hopped along the boulder on which it had landed, cawed a few times and then waited.

A lone figure appeared on the fringe of the jungle. It looked like a goblin, but was a good deal smaller and possessed of a nose that was at least twice as big as a goblin's. Its entire skin looked as though it had been dripped on and melted down. Everything appeared to be . . . *glutinous*.

Burnie waddled over to the ravensage, and unclipped the scroll from its leg. Unfurling the parchment, he began to read:

> *Burnie,*
> *Danger worse than at first imagined. A dark god has arisen in Dullitch, presumably the result of the impostor's wicked wranglings. He calls himself Vanquish, commands dragons and has the power to*

*turn men into mindless gravewalkers. Groan Teethgrit has become a vessel for the fiend, who inhabits the warrior's body. We must sadly report that Nazz, our true friend, has fallen in battle. Thanks to his courage, we have escaped the city in a ship belonging to Earl Visceral. We are hoping to travel to Spittle, meet with the earl and secure his support in some way. The capital must be reclaimed.*
*Your loyal servants,*
*Spatula, Quickstint and Obegarde*
*THE SECRET ARMY OF DULLITCH*

Burnie sighed, and looked back towards the jungle.

*Desperate situations call for desperate measures*, he thought.

**'You failed me.'**

Vanquish rose from his throne and descended the steps. Gordo and Gape were kneeling on the flagstones before him, their heads bowed in shame.

'A second chance, lord,' said the spirit inhabiting Gordo, obviously uncomfortable with the voice it now possessed. 'Give us a second chance.'

'Please, lord,' added Gape's soul-occupier. 'Just one more chance.'

Vanquish said, simply: '**No.**'

He lowered his hands and two bolts of energy settled on the heads of both warriors. The energy changed colour from red to blue and back again. Then the humbled pair re-opened their eyes.

Vanquish smiled through Groan's teeth.

'**The last two failed me**,' he boomed. '**You will prove yourselves infinitely better souls, I am sure. Now leave me in peace.**'

The warriors bowed their heads once more, then rose and departed the room.

Vanquish waited for a time, then dropped to Groan's knees and began to concentrate his thoughts.

*Dragons. My very own creatures . . . my first creations. Hear me. Now.*

*We hear, dark lord. Command us.*

*You must remain on the gates.*

*We hear, and obey.*

*Good. I need more of your kind.*

*There are no more of us left. We . . . are the last.*

*I need more.*

*There are none.*

*If not here: where?*

*In the otherworld . . . maybe . . . but most of the kin are lost . . .*

*Then I will open the gate and draw them forth.*

*As you wish.*

Vanquish shifted his attention to a dark, shadowy corner of the throne room, and began to mumble an incantation.

A pocket of energy materialized in the space, swirling

around as the force of the magic made it grow.

Vanquish increased the intensity of the spell, raising his hands and shaping the doorway as it developed.

*Dragons in the depths. Hear me now. I command you: come forth.*

There was no reply, in thought or tone.

*HEAR ME NOW! I COMMAND YOU TO COME FORTH!*

Nothing.

Vanquish sighed. It was as he feared; he would have to take Illmoor by a far more circuitous route.

He rose to his feet and marched determinedly from the chamber.

The dark portal began to disintegrate behind him, fading from the room like a half-imagined mist . . . but before it vanished entirely, a thin, pale hand appeared from within, clawing frantically at the flagstones as it attempted, once, twice, three times to pull itself from the darkness. There was a barely discernable *pop* . . . and out on to the floor rolled a youth, eyes mad with tears, and black hair matted to his face. His fingernails were bleeding.

# Six

Illmoor had always consisted of two worlds: the world above and the world below. A traveller in the world above might be warned of such things as trolls, ogres, elves, dwarves and goblins, but it was always *men* that caused the trouble. In the world below, tales of wicked fairies, stride-hares and at least one mutated rabbit with a time fetish masked the real threat to anyone passing through: the troglodyte Kingdom of Ungst. Little more than a legend to the higher races, the kingdom nevertheless existed, far beneath Carafat, and literally pulsing with life. Admittedly, it was small: the hundred or so inhabiting troglodytes went about their daily business – which consisted mainly of hitting

each other with makeshift flails, and nesting.

Through these mean streets Burnie scurried, looking tired, hungry and more like a peasant than the Council Chairman of Illmoor's capital city.

*Make that ex-Chairman,* he thought. His flight from Dullitch had been an involuntary one: he'd managed to escape the clutches of Sorrell Diveal with his life, but not much else.

It was no accident that he hadn't visited his birthplace since he'd left home, some thirty years previously: in fact, he'd planned *never* to return. However, he told himself, needs must as the devil drives, and the devil was certainly driving.

As he swept through the main plaza, Burnie noticed he'd gathered a crowd that appeared to be made up of half the city's entire population. It wasn't surprising: he was still dressed in the high robes of Dullitch Council and probably looked outlandishly impressive to the rest of his species, who mainly wore loincloths and little else.

Burnie marched on determinedly, leading the snake-formation of troglodotion inquisitiveness to the very foot of King Slythi's roost.

There were no houses in Ungst: troglodytes preferred roosts. It wasn't hard to obtain a roost: you merely gathered together all your belongings . . . and sat on them. In Ungst, a king was elected at the end of each year, after measurements had been taken to discover

who sat atop the biggest pile of accumulated junk. Slythi Toe had been King of Ungst for nearly fifty years – and he was so far up that it was practically impossible to see him.

Burnie arrived at the base of the giant mound and quickly peered around for the inevitable speaker-on-a-stick. There was always such a device at the base of the larger mounds: as most troglogytes barely bothered to walk, climbing down to talk to visitors was out of the question.

'King Slythi!' Burnie bellowed into the speaker. 'It is I, Burnie, son of Hyburni and Hyburnia. I return to Ungst at a time of great peril for all.'

There was a moment of frantic scrabbling in the background as the crowd realized something big was happening and began to get comfortable.

Silence.

Burnie looked up at the mound, squinting to see if he could make out any movement on top. There was nothing.

'Did you hear me, King Slythi?' he called again. 'I said, It is I, Burnie, son of Hyburni and Hyburnia. I return to Ungst at a time of great peril for all!'

There was another long silence. Then a voice cried out:

'I know who speak. What want you?'

Burnie took a deep breath: it had been so long, he'd almost forgotten the ignorance inherent in his race.

'I need your help!' he screamed. 'The city of Dullitch is in dire peril: a terrible enemy has arisen! You must assist those above ... or ALL will be lost to darkness.'

An echo died away with the words.

'You leave here long ago, Burnie, son of Hyburni,' boomed the reply. 'You no come back long time. You *them* now: you no us. You high them; you *robe.*'

As the crowd gave a collective sneer, the little troglodyte rolled his eyes and raised the speaker once more to his rubbery lips. He was going to have to speak to the king in his own language.

'Listen me!' he screamed. 'I you more them! Me no you soon, you no you longer! You no you for great evil come! Me no you save, you no me save. All perish in black fire! Vanquish you know me know you know. Vanquish enemy old! Vanquish walk in giant step back up top. Bad: you know me know! Teethgrit legend tribe great – Teethgrit body hero Vanquish take! Groan! Groan! Groan!'

Burnie smiled as he finished: a collective gasp had risen up with his words.

'You no lie?' exclaimed the king. 'Vanquish walk Teethgrit now: you tell true?'

Burnie nodded and bellowed: 'I tell true, Slythi. I tell true. Friends mine go help seek: Visceral Earl Spittle! Others too; great army form, maybe hopes me.'

'Hopes you army great?'

'Hopes me.' Burnie nodded, squinting up at the top of the pile. 'Hopes me lots like.'

There was a commotion of some kind at the top of the pile. Several pieces of junk clattered down the heap as King Slythi came thundering down the constructed mountain. At nearly three times the size of his citizens, Slythi was a sight to behold, his scaly muscles glistening with excretions.

'Weapon want!' he slithered. 'Weapon WANT!'

Sunlight streamed into the palace, penetrating every nook, cranny and keyhole, streaming under doors and sneaking around corners.

Diek Wustapha's head swam with horrific dreams and echoed with nightmare images. He had been trapped in the black dimension for what felt like centuries, floating through darkness while the *talons* of the void clawed at his soul . . . and all because of the voices.

Diek's eyelids flickered as the light spilled over them. His mind was racing, flowing back through the hidden corridors of his subconscious, showing him the contents of all the locked drawers. How long had it been since the voice had left him? Minutes? Hours? Days? Months? It was difficult to tell. He certainly remembered its arrival: he'd been sitting in his father's field, playing a tune on . . . a tune . . . the rats . . . the children . . . Dullitch!

Diek started, shocked awake by the sudden horror of

the memory. In a blink, he saw *everything* . . . and the knowledge that came with it washed over him like a flood. The old wizard had done something . . . opened a door . . . and they had both gone through . . . into nothing.

Diek Wustapha opened his eyes . . .

. . . and found himself in what appeared to be a cupboard. A warm smile split his lips as he reached out and touched a broom-handle. The solidity of the object almost brought him to tears: this was a *real* broom, an actual, everyday wooden broom! How long had it been since he'd seen one? How long had it been since he'd actually *touched* anything?

Diek used the broom to get himself to his feet, noticing that the handle glowed in the darkness when he gripped it. He still felt dizzy, but the nightmares that had plagued him for so long had been dissolved by the arrival of a thin shaft of light, which shone through the keyhole. No more spiteful shadows, no more *dead* air.

From what little he could tell from the washy reflection in the cupboard's cracked and broken mirror, he hadn't grown old; his face was still pale and unblemished, though his eyes were strangely dark. His hair, which had always been short, dark and spiky, was now long and matted, with a single strand of white among the black.

So . . . time *had* taken its toll. But how much time . . . and where was he now? Well, *wherever* he was, he had to get home. His parents would be . . . what? Missing him? Ancient? Dead?

And then, in the blink of an eye, the world went white as the door opened and an unstoppable torrent of light streamed into the broom cupboard.

'Who the hell are you?' said a voice.

Diek, one hand covering his eyes, could just make out a pike and some tarnished armour.

'I said, who the hell are you?' the voice repeated. 'And what are you doin' in 'ere?'

The boy straightened up.

'My name is Diek Wustapha,' he muttered. 'Where is this place?'

'Dullitch Palace. How did you get in here? Are you homeless?'

'What? Er . . . no. I come from Little Irkesome . . .'

'Unlikely: that's *miles* away. How did you sneak in?'

Diek rubbed his head: he had so many questions himself; how could he answer someone else's?

'I . . . arrived here,' he managed.

'You bein' funny, kid?'

The guard stepped back, dimming the light enough for Diek to get his bearings. He'd had an awful day, so far. The palace was on high alert following the explosion, and all the senior officers had been gathered in the main courtyard for the last eighteen hours, to no apparent end. He just wasn't in the mood to let some young joker try his luck.

'*What* did you say your name was?' he prompted, flexing his knuckles.

'Diek. Diek Wustapha.'

'Ha! You were named after the rat-catcher? Your parents must have a sense of humour, I reckon.'

'Rats?' Diek looked up, suddenly. 'You remember the rats? I got rid of them!'

The guard smiled and leaned down to whisper in the boy's ear.

'Nice try, kid: but you need some serious make-up if you want to pull off a con like that. The *real* Diek Wustapha would be about my age by now . . . and anyway, if it's charity you're after, you should pretend to be someone the city actually *wants* to see. Diek Wustapha kidnapped the children of Dullitch: if he walked back into the city right now, he'd probably be 'anged.'

'He would?'

'Yeah, or worse. Now step outta that cupboard or I'll wrench ya out.'

Diek glanced sideways at the broom, which had stopped glowing but still felt oddly . . . alive.

'I – think this broom is magic,' he muttered. 'Either that, or I've brought some magic with me from the . . . place where I was before. I hope not: magic gets me into trouble.'

'Get OUT,' snapped the guard, beginning to lose his temper. 'Are you a mental patient or something?'

'It could be a wizard's broom . . . or a witch's, maybe. It feels . . . light.'

The guard rested his pike against the wall, and cracked his knuckles.

'You know what I reckon,' he growled, snatching hold of Diek and dragging both him and the broom out of the cupboard. 'I reckon you're just a crafty little street urchin who sneaked his way into the palace and got found out. Know what else I reckon? I *reckon* you're just comin' up with any old cock and bull rubbish, thinkin' I'm just some dumb guard who'll fall for everythin' you choose to tell me. Well, let's see about this magic witch's broom, shall we?' The guard lifted Diek – who was still dragging the broom – straight off his feet, and marched him over to the nearest window.

'We're three floors up,' he muttered. 'So this here magic broom is *just* what the surgeon ordered, eh?'

He hoisted Diek over his head and threw him, bodily, out of the window.

The boy scrabbled on the air for a millisecond before he plunged, kicking and screaming, towards the ground. He snatched out at the broom as it plunged with him.

''Ere, quick,' the guard snorted at a second sentry, who was approaching the window. 'Come and see thi—'

His words died away as he looked back into the courtyard . . . where the broom had paused in midair, Diek still clutching on to it for dear life. There were a few twists and spins, and then the boy, broom firmly

beneath him, rocketed back towards the window. Both guards ducked instinctively as the missile flew over them into the room . . . and then they regained enough sense to give chase.

# Seven

A meandering queue of troglodytes snaked away from the little recruiting-table. Burnie couldn't help but smile: his people might not be smart, but they were brave, loyal, quick and always, always up for a fight.

A particularly sturdy-looking example of the breed arrived before the recruitment officer.

'I'm join,' he croaked.

The officer looked up through jellied eyes. 'Join you now want?'

'I'm join,' the volunteer confirmed.

'Flail you?'

'Me flail. See.'

The warrior brandished a nasty looking, three-whipped flail.

'Flail good. Who you?'

There was a lengthy period of silence.

The officer paused, looked up again.

'Who you, I say?'

'Me him brother.'

'Him brother?'

The officer glanced over at a second, fat troglodyte and pointed a gnarly finger. 'Him brother, you say?'

'Him brother mine.'

'One next!'

The recruit shuffled off, and the line moved on.

'I'm join.'

'Flail you?'

'Me flail.'

'Who you?' came the (by now, predictable) question.

'Me him son.'

Burnie watched the proceedings with an increasingly doubtful expression. He tried to express his worries in troglodotion, but ended up resorting to plain tongue.

'Are you sure these army lists are going to make sense?' he muttered, turning to King Slythi. 'I mean, there's not a single *name* on there: how are you going to do things like roll-call?'

The king gave him a look of defiance.

'Weapon need,' he snarled, brandishing a scimitar. 'Weapon have.'

Burnie nodded.

'I think I understand. When this . . . enlisting procedure is done, do you think we may be able to head for Spittle?'

'Spittle no see, Dullitch danger.'

Burnie sighed.

'Yes, I know *that*, Slythi,' he managed. 'But we need to join with *others*, we need to form a great army! Vanquish is incredibly powerful: only together can we see this through!'

'Spittle no go,' Slythi snapped. 'Dullitch go. Dullitch go!'

Burnie muttered something under his breath, but continued to smile. Nevertheless, as the queue of volunteers moved on, he tried the path of reason once more.

'Look, King Slythi, there's not ENOUGH of you to go straight to Dullitch! A hundred trogs against a dark god? It's insane.'

'Say you trogs!' Slythi bared his pointed teeth. 'Say you trogs and one you: one you!'

'I know *that*,' said Burnie, guiltily. 'Look, I didn't mean to use the slang term . . . I'm just worried that you're all going to get wiped out. If you let me lead the group to Spittle, maybe we can join forces with Earl Visceral . . . That way, we might actually stand a

chance of saving Illmoor from this . . . thing.'

Slythi looked down at his sword, then at the thin line of volunteers standing beside the table.

'Think I,' he muttered. 'Think I now.'

Burnie nodded.

'Let me know what you decide,' he said, hopefully, turning back to the table.

'Think I done,' Slythi snapped, suddenly. 'Long think I done.'

Burnie's jaw dropped.

'That was quick!' he said.

'Quick think me.'

'I'll say. So . . . what's your decision?'

The king looked down at his sword, then back at Burnie, his teeth gleaming in the fiery glow of the underdark.

'Dullitch go!' he screamed. 'Dullitch go! Dullitch go!'

The exhalation got a roar of approval from the recruits . . . and a sigh of despair from Burnie.


The enchanted broom was heading for the ground like a rogue dart. Diek tried to close his eyes against the rush of wind, but the memory of the darkness forced them open.

There was an audible *whoosh*.

. . . and the broom suddenly jerked to a standstill. Diek peered, with mounting dread, over his shoulder. His trip out again through the palace walls had evidently gained him some baggage: there was part of a bookcase hanging off the brush-end of the broom, spilling its contents to the ground.

Diek spun himself around and kicked madly at the devastated wood, desperate to lose the weight before it dragged too heavily on the unpredictable transport.

Too late.

'No! NO! *Noooooooo!*'

The broom plummeted from the sky. As he flew inexorably downwards, Diek tried to make out where he was. Far from the city, that was for sure . . . but how far could he fall before . . .

His answer came in the form of a tree, which he collided with, crashing through the branches on a long and bumpy ride to the ground. When he eventually did find the forest floor, he landed awkwardly, an unfortunately large root knocking the wind out of him.

'Urgh,' he managed, before something heavy and wooden dropped out of the lower branches and clonked him on the skull.

'Owwww!'

The boy put a hand to his aching head, but passed out before he could massage it. The jungle swam around him . . . and he dreamed again.

During his childhood, Diek's dreams had consisted of the usual, everyday rubbish: fairies playing the drums, a man in a black suit picking his nose with a garden-fork, pigs dancing, etc. Now, however, these whimsical

fantasies were thinning . . . and Diek *did* manage to wonder, rather vacantly, just how long he'd been in the hellish limbo that surrounded him.

For a time, the boy snored . . . and the forest around him grew dark. When he eventually awoke, it was twilight.

'My head,' he said, to no one in particular. 'My head hurts.'

'*I* carn even feel me 'ead,' said a deep and very menacing voice.

Diek, still oblivious to his surroundings, rolled on to his side. 'Wh-where am I? Was it all just a dream? Am I still in that . . . *place*?'

'Dunno. Don' ask me. I carn see nuffin'.'

'I know how *that* feels. It doesn't seem like much of a—' Diek's eyes flicked open and he sat bolt upright. He was in a dark, shadowy jungle and, more importantly, he was alone. A quick glance in every direction turned up nothing more than a few oddly shaped plants and some debris from the bookcase. Diek looked up: the broom was still wedged in the higher branches of the tree.

'Insane,' he muttered. 'I've been enchanted, imprisoned in a black void, heard voices, and now I've gone insane; had to happen. Understandable, really; all things considered.' He waited a few seconds to make sure the voice wasn't going to comment, then climbed unsteadily to his feet.

'I hate these places,' he complained to himself,

getting comfortable with his new lunacy. 'Nothing but black shadows, screeching sounds and things that slither.'

'An' spiders.'

'Well, of course; spiders go without saying. There's probably hun—'

Diek stopped short, and turned his head slightly. 'Who said that?' he demanded. 'Is there somebody else here with me? Somebody *real?*'

'Yeah – me.'

'Are you real?'

'Always fort so.'

'Are you . . . invisible?'

'Dunno. Am I?'

Diek spun on his heels and hurried around the clearing, checking in bushes and behind the wider trees.

'You seem to be,' he admitted, at last. 'The problem is that you're a voice . . . and I've heard voices before. They're never a good sign.'

'Who are ya, then?'

'My name is Diek.'

'I've 'eard that name 'fore.'

'Oh.'

'You dun' soun' surprised. Famous, are ya?'

Diek shook his head.

'Not really,' he muttered. 'But I once did something bad that . . . attracted a lot of attention. Not on purpose, mind: I was enchanted!'

'Yeah? I 'tract 'tention all the time. I once rescued an 'tire, city o' kids from some young 'chanter what took umbrage when he wasn't paid for killin' rats. Did they fank me? Did they 'ell.'

'Yes, well I expect . . .' Diek's voice trailed away and he froze. The jungle around him seemed to grow even darker. Then, speaking very quickly, he said: 'Er . . . who *are* you, exactly?'

There was a moment of silence in which, Diek fancied, he could actually *hear* the voice thinking.

'Name's Groan Teethgrit. I'm a famous warrior, me.'

'I . . . er . . . think we may have met.'

'You an' me?'

'Yes.'

'When?'

'A few years ago.'

'Where?'

'A tavern in Dullitch called the Rotting Ferret.'

'Sounds 'bout right. Did I beat y'up?'

'I don't think so; I seem to recall that you and your dwarf friend helped me . . . then again, I was in a bit of a daze.' Diek's memory was giving him some frightening updates. 'I think we probably met again, not long after that . . . you might have tried to kill me *then* . . . but it was probably for all the right reasons.'

'I've killed folk jus' for lookin' at me.'

Diek nodded and peered around him.

'Well, changing the subject, Mr Teethgrit,' he said,

'you don't actually seem to be a warrior any more. In fact, you don't actually seem to be *anything*.'

'D'ya wanna make somefing of it?'

Diek bit his lip, and took a deep breath. 'I didn't mean to upset you,' he whispered. 'I'm just saying what I see, and I can't see *anything*. You're just a voice in my head! What happened to you?'

'Dunno; can't 'member tha' much.'

Diek approached his next question with care.

'Um,' he began, his own voice shaking slightly, 'has it been a very long time since the business with the rats?'

'Dunno. What date is it now?'

Diek frowned.

'I have no idea; that's why I asked.'

Another moment flittered away in noisy thought.

'I reckon that rat stuff 'appened 'bout fifteen years ago . . .'

'Fifteen years?' Diek almost choked on his own breath. 'Fifteen YEARS?'

'Yeah . . . back 'fore I became King o' Phlegm.'

'Fifteen years . . .' Diek muttered, beginning a slow walk out of the clearing in order to try and stop his head thumping. 'Fifteen . . . that's incredible. Is Duke Modeset still on the throne of Dullitch?'

'Nah, he was chucked out over the rat stuff. I did 'im in, few years 'go. Viscount Curfew took over after 'im, only it turned out to be this uvver bloke what— oi! Where you goin? I can 'ear you movin' . . .'

'I'm heading over this way to see where—' Diek stopped short, realizing that the voice had now grown distant. 'Can't you come with me?' he called back.

'Nah, don' fink so. I carn feel me legs.'

'Hmm. Can you feel *anything* at all?'

'Nah . . . I can 'ear me voice, tho.'

Diek scratched his head and looked back towards the clearing he'd just emerged from. 'Keep talking,' he hazarded.

''Bout what?'

'Anything . . . just tell me a bit about the things that have happened to you . . . and I'll see if I can't find out where you are from your voice.'

'Yeah, all righ'.'

Groan dived into a long and, Diek had to admit, rather exciting story about disembodied corpses, forgotten cities full of zombies, battles with spider kings and various plots to destroy one lord or another. Eventually, however, he located the source of Groan's voice . . .

'You're in a box,' he said simply, picking up the small casket and examining it carefully.

'You what?'

'Your voice is coming from a box. Specifically, it's got a little grid on the front; I'm looking through it, right now: can you see my eye?'

'Nah. S'dark in 'ere.'

'Oh.' Diek turned the box over in his pale hands. 'Should I open it, do you think?'

'Dunno.'

'Well, it's *your* box . . .'

'Yeah . . . all righ'. Go on, then.'

Diek lifted the lid and peered inside.

'There's a white mist,' he said, eyeing the contents suspiciously. 'Hang on, I'll try to tip it out.'

He upended the box and shook it violently, but nothing emerged from within. After a while, he closed it again.

'Nothing happened, I'm afraid – the mist won't come out. Looks like powerful magic of some kind. Did you upset a witch or something?'

'Nah . . . don' fink so . . . but I don't 'member nothin'.'

'Mmm . . . well, either way, I think we need to get you looked at.' Diek tucked the box under his arm, then picked a random direction and began to march through the forest.

'This might take a while,' he muttered. 'I'm afraid I don't know Illmoor that well, and I don't have the slightest idea where we are . . .'

'S'all right: I'll tell ya where we are.'

Diek frowned. 'How can you? You're in a box.'

'I know me way 'round. 'Sa wood, right?'

'Um . . . it's actually more like a jungle. It's quite warm.'

'South, then. Can only be Shadewell or Car' fat. There 'ny big trees?'

'I'm sorry; what was that?'

'The trees; 'ny big ones?'

Diek looked around him. 'They're ALL big.'

'Are they fat 'an all?'

'Er . . . reasonably, I suppose.'

'Is there lots o' vines wiv blue stuff drippin' off 'em?'

'Well . . . yes!'

'An' a lot o' smashed-up statues lyin' 'bout?'

'Now that you come to mention it, I *can* see one or two . . .'

'S'Car' fat, then; you wanna 'ead east.'

'Really?'

'Yeah.'

'That's brilliant!' Diek grinned. 'Any other good advice?'

'Yeah,' said Groan. 'Never buy a moffskin coat off a bloke you only seen twice wearin' it.'

'Right,' Diek replied, weakly. 'I'll try to remember that.'

They walked along in silence for a time, Diek trying to start random conversations to avoid the awkwardness of the situation. 'Er . . . have you got a wife or children, Mr Teethgrit?'

'No' really,' Groan boomed. 'I got a boy somewhere; but I reckon they put 'im in 'idin' an' tol' 'im I was dead.'

'Why would they do that?'

'I'm not ver' 'sponsible.'

'Oh. I see.' Diek swallowed a few times and tried to think of something else to say. 'Er . . .' he began. 'Do you have anything you'd like to ask me?'

'Yeah.' Groan's voice dropped to a whisper. 'Are you that young 'chanter what took all them kids outta Dullitch?'

Diek looked down at the box.

'You catch on very fast, Mr Teethgrit,' he said.

'Fort so. The o' wizard pushed ya into tha' black 'ole an' ended up goin' in hisself. D'you 'member?'

Jimmy Quickstint had decided that he didn't like the crew of the *Royal Consort*. They were gruff, unwelcoming and very antisocial, and they certainly didn't appreciate someone teaching them how to keep hold of their belongings.

'All I'm saying,' Jimmy whispered to the captain, 'is that by wearing a bracelet loose on your wrist, you're inviting trouble. Here . . .'

He handed back the diamond-encrusted band, with a knowing wink. 'Fortunately, I'm the kind of thief who's willing to let you in on a few trade secrets. Next time, you might not be so lucky.'

The captain grimaced at him. 'Next time, I'll cut your throat with my blade.'

'Look, there's no need—'

'You just stole my bracelet, you little scumba—'

'I gave it back!'

'Yeah, because I saw you slip it off when you shook my hand.'

'Ah, yeah, but you didn't *feel* it coming off, did you?'

'Yes.'

'Liar.'

The captain drew his blade, causing Jimmy to take several steps back.

'I'd rejoin your friends, if I were you,' the captain muttered.

Jimmy rolled his eyes.

'I dunno,' he muttered, mooching up to Obegarde and slumping down on to the barrel beside him. 'You try to help people out, and all you get is a sword-edge at your throat and a mouthful of abuse.'

'Quiet!' Effigy snapped. 'Just be quiet, will you?'

Jimmy glanced at Obegarde, and sniffed. 'What's wrong with *him*?'

'The ravensage just arrived back,' said Vanya, who was still taking it upon herself to make the group feel welcome aboard her father's ship. 'I think your friend has replied.'

'What, already? Wow! What did he say?'

Obegarde, who was looking over Effigy's shoulder at a piece of paper, heaved a long sigh. 'Pretty much nothing,' he confirmed. 'All it says is: *Meet you in Spittle.*'

'Disappointing.' Effigy conceded. 'I thought at the very least he might give us some idea of what he thinks we should do.'

'Maybe he will, when he sees us,' said Obegarde. 'You know Burnie, cagey to the last.'

Vanya tried to break the growing air of despondency.

'My father will know what to do,' she assured them. 'He is totally passionate about Illmoor, believe me.'

'Yeah,' Jimmy grumbled. 'They used to say that about Modeset, and look what happened to him . . .'

# Eight

Vortain Visceral was a popular ruler, and not merely because his family had commanded Spittle since the city had first been conceived. He was angular, pale and gaunt, with a chin so pointed that many voiced the opinion that his head looked exactly like a crescent moon. Visceral was also a very strange man, and had aged little in the ninety-seven years he'd been on the throne. Some took his unnaturally long life and nocturnal demeanour to be a sign of vampiric or ghoulish pursuits, though in truth Visceral had never drunk blood and the thought of flesh-eating was abhorrent to him. Moreover, the earl had no great taste for food: he seldom even dipped a biscuit these days.

The actual fact of the matter was this: Vortain Visceral had absolutely no idea why he was the way he was . . . and he certainly didn't want to question it. If the gods had seen fit to grant him extended tenure and a body that never looked much over thirty, then who was he to disagree? Gods were whimsical creatures, after all, and to be fair, he'd always wondered if they'd given him Spittle as a form of punishment.

People said Dullitch was bad – people who'd never set foot in Spittle. Few did.

Nevertheless, like all cities, it had its good points. If you wanted to trade anything, absolutely anything at all, you went to Spittle. You just didn't expect to return with anything more than a black eye and, if you were lucky, a limp.

Today, the city was bursting with energy, activity, enthusiasm and the sort of smells that only went away after you set light to the source.

Spittle Tower, home to the royal family, was arguably the most visited site in Illmoor, due not to its particular size or questionable beauty, but because it was the continent's only *leaning* tower – if the word *leaning* could actually be applied to a building that had bent at such an angle as to practically lay horizontally across the landscape. It was also a structure surrounded by mystery – not least because the corpses of several limbo dancers were still under there somewhere.

Inevitably, the rooms inside were all slanted at a

ludicrous angle, and only Earl Visceral himself managed to walk the corridors with his dignity intact.

Today, the page on duty threw all his energy into climbing the long corridor to the throne room. When he reached the portal, he clung on for a time, before managing to swing himself into the room.

'A message for the earl,' he gasped. 'It's quite urgent.'

Earl Visceral, sitting in an ornate chair that had been nailed to the floor to stop it sliding into the far wall, looked up from his news-scroll.

'Urgent?' he snapped. 'I can't remember the last time I got an urgent message. It's not from Prince Blood, is it? Another complaint about the trade fair with Spittle I *don't* need.'

The page shook his head. 'No, Highness, it's a message from Lady Vanya: she's on the ship from Dullitch . . .'

'Ah yes. Her term will have ended.'

'. . . with a vampire and two other refugees.'

'What's that? Refugees? What are you talking about?'

The page wiped some sweat from his brow with a free hand. 'It appears that there has been some sort of an uprising in the capital. Her ladyship says that she will explain upon her arrival, but that in the meantime you must call a meeting of the High Council.'

'But—'

'It appears, Highness, that there's a very real chance that Viscount Curfew has been murdered, and that some sort of . . . *creature* now sits on the throne.'

Earl Visceral swallowed a few times. Then he did what he always did whenever he got bad news. He closed his eyes and thought on it for several minutes. Eventually, he opened them again.

'I . . . that is . . . does she say anything else?' he demanded.

'No, milord. Only that she loves you and that you mustn't do anything foolish until she arrives.'

The earl seemed to be rather resentful of the last bit, but he rose from his chair and, grasping hold of wall-mounted braziers and table edges, began to negotiate his way across the floor.

'Very well: summon the High Council.'

'Yes, Highness.'

'Not all of them, mind: invite Viceroy Funk of Shinbone, Baron Muttknuckles of Sneeze and, of course, Prince Blood. I don't want that witch from Beanstalk nosing around and you can forget calling on the shifty pair who run Crust and Chudderford these days. Have I left anybody *else* out?'

'Er . . . the Steward of Fogrise, Highness?'

'Um . . . no, don't bother. Pegrand Marshall is ill, I believe.'

'And what of Phlegm?'

'Phlegm? Oh, you can ignore them as well. Groan Teethgrit never bothers to come to HC meetings, and he's seldom in the city, anyway. Leads a life of reckless

adventure, that one. They should never have given him the throne . . .'

'Er, sorry, Highness, but I was actually talking about the *Steward* of Phlegm.'

'Oh, I see. No, then. N-O. Absolutely not.'

'Yes, but Lord Lambontroff—'

'. . . is a decapitated head on a stick. I don't care if it talks, I'm not discussing matters of national urgency with something I have to hold like a lollipop – when it's not rolling all over the cushions.'

'Very well, Highness . . . I just thought that his lordship might be a powerful ally . . .'

'In what sense? As a cannonball, perhaps?'

'No, Highness. Rumour has it that Phlegm has built up a large contingent of—'

'Yes, yes! All right, invite him – but make sure he brings his own cushions this time. It took us weeks to get the last lot clean . . .'

The page bowed low, almost falling over in the attempt, and departed.

Diek Wustapha trudged on through the damp and murky jungle.

The conversation between him and Groan had been limited, but he soon came to realize that conversations between *anyone* and Groan were limited. The man had only two topics on which he would openly comment: money and hand-to-hand combat. Since Diek was interested in neither, he'd decided to remain quiet and hope that his companion would do the same. Unfortunately, luck wasn't with him for long.

''Ere,' said Groan. 'Where'd you come from?'

'Orginally? A place called Little Irkesome.'

'Bin there. I beat up some bloke what owed me ten crowns.'

'Oh . . . good.'

'Yeah, was.'

'I . . . er . . . didn't come from there *today*, though.'

'Eh?'

'When we met, back there in the jungle, I had just come from Dullitch. Some guards tried to arrest me, but I found a magic broom and escaped from the palace.'

'Good on ya. I 'ad a magic broom once.'

'You? Really?'

'Yeah, got twenny crowns for it off some bloke up in Sneeze. I ended up kickin' his bruvver fru a door 'cause he didn' pay up.'

Diek rolled his eyes.

'Right. Of course you did – back when you were a bit more than a disembodied voice. So what's the *last* thing you remember from those times, then?'

There was a definite pause, before Groan's monotonous voice rolled on.

'I 'member this 'ammer that turned out to be a key an' the wizard what made himself look like Viscount Curfew an' put hisself on the throne, he tells me 'bout

the secret treasure an' so I go up to unlock it an' Gordo
– s'me mate – says I shouldn' do it, but I does it anyway
an' then . . . er . . . I dunno what happened 'fter that.'

'It all sounds very complicated,' said Diek, doubtfully.
'But I'm guessing something happened to you when you
unlocked the thing your friend told you not to
unlock . . .'

'Yeah, must've done.'

'I hope your friend is OK.'

'Don' worry 'bout him,' Groan's voice boomed.
'He's tough as nails, is Gordo. 'Sides, he's got me bruvva
wiv 'im.'

'Good. So tell me . . . where are we going, exactly?'

'Dullitch.'

'I see.' Diek allowed a couple of minutes to drift by in
silence. Then he said: 'Er . . . is that wise?'

''Ow d'you mean?'

'Well, it's just that you said there was a wizard on
the throne.'

'So what?'

'So . . . if he's changed you into a-a-a voice in a box,
he must be pretty powerful!'

'I can kill 'ny wizard goin', me.'

'Yes, I believe you probably could have – back when
you were, well, *you*. But it's different now, isn't it? You're
just a voice in a box and, as such, it's pretty stupid to go
walking back into the city, isn't it?'

'You callin' me stupid?'

'No! I'm just saying that maybe we should think about things first, that's all. Besides, I have your box, so it's up to me really.'

'We're goin' to Dullitch.'

'I don't think—'

'We're goin' to Dullitch or else.'

Diek stopped dead, glaring down at the box.

'Or else what? What exactly do you think you're going to do? Mist me up?'

'I'll kick yer teeth out the back of yer 'ead.'

'Go on then!'

'I'm gonna.'

'GO ON THEN! DO IT!' Diek waited a few seconds, his teeth clenched in anticipation. 'You can't, can you?'

Silence.

'Well, can you?'

More silence.

'Right, then. So you can just shut up: *I'll* decide where we're going.'

'Just make sure it's somewhere you don' mind bein' buried.'

'I think,' Diek started, ignoring the last remark, 'that we should go and see my parents. Yes, that's where we'll go – back to Little Irkesome.' He smiled at the thought. 'Which way is it?'

'Dunno.'

'Oh, come on. Don't be immature: just tell me.'

'Nah, I don' 'member.'

'If you don't tell me, I'm going to put your box down and leave you here.'

'You wouldn' dare.'

'Try me.'

Diek smiled to himself and crouched down to deposit the box on the jungle floor. He was preparing to demonstrate the second part of his bluff, when he heard the sound of marching feet: lots of them.

Diek quickly regained his footing and spun around, just as the vanguard of the troglodyte warband came into view.

# Nine

Gordo and Gape marched mindlessly through the deserted streets of Dullitch, two giant caskets suspended on a chain between them. Their master's orders had been clear: they were to knock on every door in the city, draw out every able-bodied man and remove his soul. This was achieved by dunking their heads into the smaller casket, waiting until their souls were expelled, then performing the same procedure with the second casket in order for them to receive their new inhabitants.

Vanquish had explained that the deposit and imprisonment of the old souls was necessary in order to hold sway over the victim's bodies. If the body died, the soul would be released.

*However*, the dark god's voice still rang in their ears, *be certain to make the exchange swift – a body left too long vacated will automatically attract the return of its true soul.*

The citizens would resist, of course: both dark servants were looking forward to that. These people were weak, after all, and there were *thousands* of them.

Above them, the great dragons flapped noisily, their presence a deterrent to even the most determined of rebels. One by one, the people of Dullitch would be subdued. In due course, they would rise up and fight for their new master . . .


Diek Wustapha dived behind a nearby tree and crouched as low to the floor of the jungle as his fear of insects would allow.

'I knew you wouldn' 'ave the guts to leave me,' Groan's voice bragged.

'Shhh!'

'Don' shhh me.'

'There's an army coming through!'

'Eh?'

'An army, on the march: I can see them!'

'How many?'

'I'm not sure. Looks to be . . . about a hundred or so.'

'Ha! That ain't no army! Thass a warband.'

'Yeah well, army, warband: whatever, they're armed.'

'What are they, orcs?'

'I don't think so: they look smaller, and sort of rubbery.'

'Sounds like goblins t'me. What weapons they got?'

Diek squinted to make out what the warriors were carrying.

'It looks like some sort of whip with funny balls on the end.'

'Hmm . . . troglodytes, then. Weird: I ain't seen none o' them for donkey's. Which way they 'eadin'?'

'The same way we are, by the looks of it.'

'Reckon you can attack one 'n' steal his armour?'

'No!'

'Didn' fink so. Best you follow 'em, then.'

Diek glanced despondently at the passing marchers, then waited a few minutes and crept along in their wake.

'What if they're about to go to war or something?' he whispered, desperately trying to avoid the more crackly of the twigs that cluttered the path.

'They are, prob'ly. I ain't never 'eard of an army marchin' to peace.'

'Good point.'

Diek tried to sneak a little closer to the last rank of troops, but found his confidence shaken when two of the creatures repeatedly glanced back towards him. It was as if they had second sight!

'Don' let 'em get 'way,' Groan grumbled.

Diek mouthed a silent curse at the box, but continued to trail after the marchers, being careful to

distance himself from the back pair, whom he now strongly suspected were psychic.

'Whass 'app'nin' now?' asked Groan.

'Shhh: nothing!'

'TELL ME WHASS 'APP'NIN'!'

'All right! I can't see at the moment; I need to—'

Diek suddenly stopped talking: a troglodyte had stepped out of the trees and was standing in front of him, a bemused expression on its face.

'Let me give you some advice, kid,' it said, as the warband shuffled to a halt. 'When you're following people, it's really best not to TALK IN A LOUD VOICE . . . because the people you're following tend to hear you.'

Diek didn't know what to say. He looked down at the box.

'See what you've done now? I told you to be quiet!'

'Yeah, an' I tol' you I'd kick yer stinkin—'

'Er . . . HELLO,' said Burnie, waving a hand between the boy's face and the box he was carrying. 'I'm still here, in case you haven't noticed.'

'Oh, yes,' Diek replied, his face flushed with embarrassment. 'Sorry.'

'Why are you following us?'

The boy looked down at the box again, but no voice came from within.

'We . . . I . . . was just walking through . . .'

'The Carafat Jungles,' Burnie finished. 'Pound for

pound, the most inhospitable pocket of terrain in the whole of Illmoor. Out for a stroll, were you?'

'No! I . . . we . . .'

'You keep saying we, I notice. Who's in the box, a demon of some sort?'

'Who you call in' a demon, trogsnot?'

Burnie stared fixedly at the box.

'I don't know – who *am* I talking to, exactly?'

'Gr—'

'I'm Diek Wustapha,' came the unexpected interruption. 'Very pleased to meet you, Mister . . . ?'

'Burnie,' said Burnie, taking the boy's free hand and shaking it vigorously. 'I take it you're not *the* Diek Wustapha?' he added. 'As in, the evil sorcerer who kidnapped the children of Dullitch . . . hahahaaha!'

Diek thought for a moment, then decided to plump for honesty.

'Actually,' he said, 'I am.'

The troglodyte's grin remained.

'You are . . . ?'

'Diek Wustapha. Though, to be honest, I don't actually feel all that evil.'

'But you are the rat-catcher?'

'Yes.'

'The rat-catcher who mysteriously showed up in Dullitch, rid the city of rats, then came back for all the children.'

'I was under the influence of some very dark magic at the time.'

'I know *that*,' said Burnie, hurriedly. 'I was just starting out on my first council job when it all happened. Aren't you a little . . . young to be Diek Wustapha?'

'I've been . . . in an alternate dimension,' the boy explained.

Burnie flashed him a disbelieving smile.

'Yeah, yeah,' he muttered. 'Well, Mr *Wustapha*, please stop following us – or you're going to end up having a very bad day.'

The little troglodyte turned and began to walk away.

'You don't believe me, do you?' Diek yelled after him. 'I'm sick of nobody believing me when I'm telling the truth! I am Diek Wustpha, damn it, and I really *have* been trapped in an alternate dimension!'

'Of course you have!'

'It's TRUE! I was released earlier today, when someone opened a portal at Dullitch Palace. I escaped on a magic broom, and ended in loads of trouble I didn't go looking for . . . again! If you don't believe me, ask Groan Teethgrit: he's inside this box!'

Burnie stopped dead in his tracks, and slowly turned around.

'*What* did you say?'

When the *Royal Consort* dropped anchor at Spittle Harbour, a carriage was already waiting for Lady Vanya.

She nodded to the footman and climbed inside hurriedly, followed by Effigy, Jimmy and Obegarde. Horses were urged into a trot, and the carriage began to move.

'My father never wastes time,' she said. 'I don't doubt that he has probably sent for the other lords already.'

'A relief, to be sure,' said Effigy, sagging slightly in his seat. The coach had picked up speed and was now practically rocketing through the crowded streets of Spittle.

'Do you think he will let us in on the meeting?' Jimmy asked, expecting the answer 'no'.

'Oh, absolutely,' said Vanya. 'I have told him to expect you as *special guests*. Besides, my father will value your intricate knowledge of the capital. He's a very wise man.'

'Er . . . not to be rude,' said Jimmy, 'but how do you know I've got an intricate knowledge of the capital?'

Vanya shrugged. 'You're a thief, aren't you?'

'Actually, he's a gravedigger,' said Obegarde, with a crafty smile. 'But let's just say that, from time to time, he inexplicably finds himself in other people's houses.'

Jimmy glared at him.

'Well, I'm sure you will all be valued as advisors, nevertheless.'

'I hope so,' said Effigy, his voice on the verge of exhaustion. 'I don't think I've got the energy to escape from another city.'

The group arrived at Spittle Tower, where Vanya departed to one of the many outbuildings while the rest of them were quickly ushered inside (though not before Obegarde had voiced his astonishment at the sight of the structure). The tower's inner door creaked open and the trio was met by two royal pages and an old man who turned out to be the tower's ageing caretaker: he immediately noted their expressions of disbelief.

'I take it none of you have ever visited the greatest wonder on Illmoor?' he said, yawning afterwards.

'Er . . . never,' Effigy confirmed. 'And, to be honest, I can't believe anyone can li—'

'I've been here before,' said Jimmy suddenly, causing everyone to turn and stare at him.

Effigy raised an eyebrow. 'You have?'

'Yeah. I . . . did a few jobs here, in my youth. Actually, I—'

'Yes, well, probably the less said about that, the better,' Obegarde interrupted, turning back to the old man. 'You were about to say something?'

'I was,' said the caretaker, with a sigh. 'You need to be particularly careful when walking these halls. As you can see, they slant somewhat, and it is very easy to damage your lower back if you don't hold on to the ring-pulls that line the walls – like this one.' He took hold of an iron circle and tugged on it. 'Do you understand the concept?'

Jimmy, Obegarde and Effigy all shared a glance.

'I think so,' said the vampire.

'Good. You may proceed.'

The pages bowed before the old man, as if they were going through some sort of ritual, and began to climb up the corridor. Effigy and Jimmy followed close behind, with a sniggering Obegarde bringing up the rear.

'So how old is this place?' said Effigy, conversationally.

The second page didn't turn around.

'Four hundred years,' he muttered.

'Really?' Effigy spluttered. 'Ha! And it's been at this angle the whole time?'

'No. It started to lean approximately one hundred and fifty years ago, and has gradually moved closer to the ground over the last twenty years. It is an . . . unfortunate, yet beautiful construct. Ah – here we are . . .'

They arrived at a set of double doors in the east wall. Keeping one hand wedged firmly inside the iron ring, the leading page reached over and flung open the portal.

'Your visitors have arrived, Earl Visceral,' he announced, making a leap for the ring on the other side of the corridor so that he could clear a path for the group's entrance. His colleague quickly joined him.

'Ah . . . very good,' came a loud reply from within the room. 'Do have them come in.'

'I might have to fly,' Obegarde whispered. His words provoked a none-too-friendly glare from the

two pages, who didn't appreciate their workplace being mocked.

Effigy was the first to work his way inside, and was pleasantly surprised to see that the throne room possessed a much kinder slant. He managed to half slide, half scramble his way to a chair, and quickly sat in it, relieved to find that it was nailed to the floor. He gave an audible sigh of relief.

'I must apologise for the agility required to visit me in my humble home,' said Earl Visceral, his voice ringing with sincerity. 'I do forget how it must feel at first, having got so used to the place myself.'

'Not a problem at all, your Majesty,' Effigy replied, ignoring the struggles of his two friends as they fought to get to their own chairs. 'I am Effigy Spatula, a resident of Dullitch and the spokesperson for our small group.'

'I see. Well, before we go into the details of this terrible business, perhaps you will be kind enough to introduce your friends?'

'Of course. This is Jimmy Quickstint; thief, gravedigger and resident of Dullitch.'

'Charmed, I'm sure – as long as you're not planning to bury or steal from any of my residents.'

Jimmy smiled weakly. 'Of course not, Majesty.'

'Jareth Obegarde,' Effigy continued. 'A vampire detective and resident of Dullitch.'

Earl Visceral nodded. 'Now you I *have* heard of.'

'Really?'

'Indeed; you were instrumental in the rescue of Viscount Curfew from his kidnappers, were you not?'

'Er . . . well, yes, but—'

'So was I!' Jimmy interrupted. 'So how come you haven't heard of me?' He muttered something under his breath, then appeared to remember who he was talking to, and added: 'Sorry, Majesty.'

Earl Visceral seemed to find the outburst amusing, and was trying to stifle a smirk.

'While we've chanced upon the subject of Viscount Curfew's kidnapping,' Effigy said, not relishing the long story that lay ahead of him, 'it is the firm belief of our friend and colleague, Burnie, that Viscount Curfew never returned from his kidnapping . . . and was killed during the event.'

Earl Visceral looked suddenly confused.

'Then who has been sitting on the throne?' he said. 'And who have I been having trade dinners with for the past year? An impostor? You can't seriously—'

'We do, your Majesty. I have seen the impostor's true face, and his identity is no longer a mystery: he is a sorcerer called Sorrell Diveal.'

Earl Visceral opened and closed his mouth several times, then reached for a goblet and unclipped a makeshift lid in order to drink from it.

'Sorrell Diveal is my cousin,' he said, after the third gulp.

'Yes, your Majesty: we understand that Lord Diveal

was a disgraced noble who studied sorcery and disappeared in mysterious circumstances when—'

'You're absolutely CERTAIN that Diveal has returned? You've seen him, unmasked, you say?'

'Yes, Majesty,' Effigy managed. He went on, choosing his words with care, 'We also believe him to be responsible for the murder of your other cousin, Viscount Curfew. But, begging your Majesty's pardon, I'm afraid the situation has become much, much worse . . .'

Earl Visceral replaced his goblet, and steeled himself.

'My daughter mentioned something about dragons . . .'

'If only that were the sole peril,' Effigy continued. 'The fact of the matter is that Sorrell Diveal, whether by chance or true intention, has somehow managed to release a terrible being from the void.'

'Please – continue . . .'

Effigy looked to Obegarde to take up the story.

'Basically,' the vampire muttered, 'we think – and it *is* only a series of suspicions at present – that Diveal has released this . . . thing . . . into the body of Groan Teethgrit.'

'Teethgrit!' Earl Visceral licked his lips and swallowed a few times. 'The King of Phlegm has become a vessel for a dark entity?'

'It gets worse yet,' Jimmy warned. 'Groan's brother, Gape, and his companion, dwarf mercenary Gordo

Goldeaxe, now serve him as some breed of grave-walking personal bodyguards.'

'B-but how did Groan Teethgrit and his team come to be in the palace in the first place?'

'We don't know,' Jimmy admitted, taking up the story. 'But soon after the trouble started, Effigy, myself and a few others marched a crowd to the gates, in rebellion.'

'We were met by the fiend himself,' Obegarde added. 'Along with two obsidian dragons, who pretty much cleared the grounds of everyone except Effigy.'

Earl Visceral raised an eyebrow at the freedom fighter.

'Oh, it wasn't bravery,' Effigy assured him. 'I thought they were an illusion of some sort . . . until I felt the heat from their breath.'

'This . . . dark lord . . . has a name, I assume?'

Effigy nodded. 'He called himself Vanquish.'

'Yeah,' agreed Jimmy. 'His voice was weird too: it definitely wasn't Groan's, that's for sure.'


'Tell the truth, boy! Tell the truth!'

The troglodyte warband surrounded Diek Wustapha, who was beginning to feel like an insect in a jar.

'I am!' Diek screamed. 'Groan Teethgrit IS in this box, I swear it!'

'Groan Teethgrit is nearly eight feet tall!' Burnie yelled back.

'It's just his mind that's in here, then, or something . . . I'm TELLING YOU, he's in—'

'Don't waste our time, boy! We haven't got all day to stand here deliberating with you about—'

'Right! That's it!' Diek put the box on the jungle floor and tapped on it. 'Groan? Groan! Speak! Say something to let them know you're in there.'

Silence: the barbarian didn't make a sound.

Burnie smiled humourlessly.

'Listen, boy,' he said, slowly. 'You're really, seriously beginning to annoy me.'

'But he's only keeping quiet because we had this argument about Dullitch and he wants to get me back.'

Burnie gritted his teeth.

'Look, there's something serious going on in Dullitch, and Groan Teethgrit is right in the middle of it, so don't be telling me that—'

''Ow can I be causin' trouble in Dullitch when I'm in 'ere?' said a voice; it was loud, clear and dim.

'G-Groan Teethgrit?' Burnie exclaimed, silencing the sudden clamour of troglodyte voices with a raised hand. 'King Groan of Phlegm? Is that you?'

'Yeah, 'sme.'

Burnie rubbed his forehead.

'What are you doing in the box?'

'Nuffin' much; bit o' thinkin' . . . but that didn' take too long. Now I'm jus' waitin' fer this boy ta get me back ta Dullitch.'

'Why?' Burnie asked. 'You think Vanquish will willingly give back your body?'

'Eh? Who's Vanquish?'

'The dark god who was released when—'

'I 'member a wizard.'

'Sorrell Diveal! He was an impostor . . .'

'Yeah! He looked jus' like Curfew, 'til his face came off.'

Burnie eyed the box; he was beginning to look hopeful. 'Do you recall anything else, King Teethgrit?'

'Yeah; I 'member a magic door,' said Groan suddenly, causing Burnie to lean towards the box in concentration. 'I 'member turnin' this 'ammer an' then watchin' meself from the back of me 'ead. I wen' over an' . . .'

There was a moment of dreadful silence.

'Oh no,' said Groan, sadly. 'I fink I might've 'urt Gordo.'


The door to the throne room opened, and Vanya Visceral walked in. To the group's surprise, she was standing upright.

'Hookboots,' she explained, pointing down at her footwear. 'They're a pain to get on, but they *do* grab the flagstones.' She smiled. 'I'd certainly recommend them for the more seasoned corridor climber.'

Earl Visceral smiled, but all the humour had vanished from his face. 'Welcome home, Vanya. Your friends were

just telling me of the awful business in Dullitch.'

Vanya nodded. 'We have to do something, Father. We—'

'You do, Majesty,' Effigy cut in. 'If this . . . thing has taken control of the capital, it won't be long before he sets his sights north.'

'I see that,' Visceral agreed. 'But I still have some questions for you. This friend you mention – Burnie, was it?'

'Yes: a troglodyte. He was, until recently, Chairman of Dullitch City Council, a position he had held since the time of the Yowler Uprising.'

'Ah . . . I see. And where is he now – dead?'

'No, Majesty.' Effigy shook his head. 'Burnie escaped the palace, and indeed the city, when he unmasked the truth. I sent word to him of our planned meeting with you, and that we are in dire need of his help. It is my belief he will make his way here.'

'Burnie's a rock, your Majesty,' Jimmy commented. 'You'll like him.'

'I'm sure to.' Earl Visceral set his face in a grim smile. 'But I must warn you, gentlemen, that I have absolutely no intention of sending my army to face off against two dragons. That would make me nothing more than a murderer myself.'

Effigy rolled his eyes. 'But what about—'

'Please let me finish. I have summoned the High Council, as you suggested. The lords of Shinbone and

Sneeze will come, representing the interests of the southern towns, but Prince Blood, ruler of Legrash, has a grand army . . . and Phlegm may also join our cause.'

'Phlegm?' Effigy exclaimed. 'Against its own king?'

'Well, once we explain that it is *not* their king, Steward Lambontroff may acquiesce . . .'

'Possibly.' Effigy cast a worried glance at Obegarde and Jimmy, who were looking equally concerned. 'But what about the dragons and Vanquish himself? We need to raise an army!'

Earl Visceral folded his arms and let out a deep sigh.

'I agree that an army will be required in order to take back the capital,' he said. 'But dragon killing is a job for barbarians and mercenaries . . . and from what you tell me, the best three of those in Illmoor are already working for the other side . . .'

Effigy shook his head in despair. 'Are there no wizards you can call on?'

'I know of none that remain.'

'What about the ice giants?'

'That race has been extinct for many years.'

'Orcs, goblins . . . ?'

'Only work for themselves.'

'What about the two men you hired last month, Father?' Vanya said, patiently. 'The ones that killed all the trollkin?'

Earl Visceral's gaze travelled from his daughter's

innocent expression to the looks of astonishment on the faces of his guests.

'You have two warriors up here who can kill trolls,' Effigy gasped, 'and you didn't think to mention that?'

Earl Visceral dismissed the question with a wave of his hand.

'Well, I'm still a little hazy on exactly where they came from,' he muttered. 'One was the archetypal barbarian, all muscled up and with a jaw you could ski off. The other one . . . I didn't like very much. He was quiet and I got the feeling he wasn't . . . quite the ticket.'

'Where are they now?'

'They were heading west – apart from that, I have no idea. It's probably just as well: such people are at best unreliable, at worst downright dan—'

'If you have names to go with the direction they're travelling, we could send word to the local towns and villages,' Jimmy ventured. 'Some scouts can find just about anyone, given a name . . . I know *I* could.'

Earl Visceral gripped the arms of his throne. 'Look,' he snapped. 'I've just told you . . .'

'Thungus,' Vanya announced. 'The barbarian was called Grid Thungus. He wasn't very smart; he told us all that he travelled from town to town, killing trolls and giants, and fighting for the highest bidder. His friend didn't say much, but I always got the feeling that he was the brains of the group: he was very strong, too. I saw him throw two men through a brick wall, down at the tavern. He wore a green cloak, as well – he was always covered up.'

Earl Visceral winced, but the rest of the group were mesmerized by this information.

'Do you remember *his* name, by any chance?' Effigy asked.

Vanya frowned with the effort of recollection.

'I'm not absolutely certain,' she said. 'No one was actually allowed to *ask* his name, but I'm sure I overheard the barbarian referring to him as Moltenoak.'

# Part Two
# Moltenoak

# One

Fire consumed the barrowbird, and it fell in a flaming mess of feathers from its perch.

Moltenoak sighed.

'I don't like to be reminded of my name,' he muttered, walking around the dead avian. 'It brings back . . . *memories.*'

The hill stretched on before him, all the way out of Cambleton Valley. Up there somewhere was the legendary Charney Rise, a view that was said to take in most of Grinswood and even afforded a glimpse of distant Fogrise.

*He* would be up there too, of course, but then every positive came with a negative these days . . . and he *was* company, of a sort.

Moltenoak took one glance back at the dead wolves, shifting his gaze from the sprawled carcasses to the still smouldering remains of the barrowbird.

*Fire and death,* he thought. *Just like the old days.*

He climbed on, snatching up a stick from the path as he went. It wasn't that he needed the walking aid; he just felt that a traveller in these hills would be *expected* to have a stick . . . and he certainly didn't want to attract any more hostile attention.

Too late.

'Oi!' came a cry from the edge of the woods. 'You there! Halt!'

Moltenoak rolled his eyes, and craned round to get a glimpse of the figure emerging from the trees. It was tall, broad and incredibly muscular, and it carried a double-handed axe. It could have been one of any number of northern barbarians but for the network of scars and the patchy ginger beard.

Moltenoak turned from the warrior and continued up the path. 'Oh,' he muttered. 'It's you.'

Grid Thungus took two giant leaps forward and blocked his companion's path. His lopsided grin preceded an extended palm and a raised, quizzical eyebrow. 'Well?'

Moltenoak looked down at the barbarian's open hand, then up at the man himself. 'What do you want?'

'The twenty crowns you owe me!'

'For what?'

'The bet!' Thungus made a clicking sound with his tongue. 'Or have you forgotten already?'

'The *bet*,' Moltenoak growled, 'was that I couldn't walk through the village of Charney without encountering any major problems.'

'Yeah, and you were attacked by a pack of werewolves!'

'But they *didn't* cause me a problem.'

'You were still attacked!'

'That's beside the point . . . I emerged unscathed, and I still win the bet. Therefore, it is *you* who owes *me* twenty crowns.'

Thungus sniffed. 'You'll get your twenty crowns, don't worry. I know what your lot are like when it comes to gold.'

'There is no "my lot",' Moltenoak pointed out. 'There was only ever *me*.'

Thungus muttered something under his breath, and the two companions moved on through the hills.

'Where're we heading, anyway?' the barbarian grumbled. 'There's nothing beyond these hills except Grinswood Forest, and we really don't want to be trudging through that *dump*.'

Moltenoak sighed. 'Where, then?' he complained. 'I'm definitely not going back to Spittle.'

'Why not? We're practically heroes there!'

'I told you already: I don't want the attention. I want to go somewhere . . . quiet.'

'How about Legrash?'

'THAT isn't quiet!'

'Fine,' Thungus agreed. 'In that case, we'll go to Beanstalk: it's a stopping point for all kinds of creatures, plus it's known for its congenial atmosphere: They reckon that during the Dual Age, a princess—'

'. . . got trapped in Beanstalk Tower by a giant. Yes, I know that. I was there.'

Thungus raised his eyebrows, but he didn't look that surprised. 'Killed it, did you?'

'No,' said Moltenoak, quietly. 'But I certainly gave it something to think about.'

'How old *are* you, exactly?'

'As old as I feel.' Moltenoak peered up at the gloomy sky, and shuddered. 'And I feel terrible.'

A crack of thunder split the silence, and a fine rain began to fall from the sky.

'You realize, of course, that heading for Beanstalk means we have to go back through Charney?' Thungus produced an infuriating grin. 'S'alright,' he said. 'I'll deal with the werewolves this time.'

# Two

A great army of the possessed gathered in Oval Square. They were greeted by Vanquish, who strode between the palace gates, mouthing something silently. He spoke no actual words, though every man and boy could hear him as clearly as if he was standing right next to them, whispering into their ears.

**Listen, now. The time has come for my loyal servants to dominate Illmoor once again. Turn now, and face the city gates, secure in the knowledge that I am with you.**

He turned to the vast swarm of heads that occupied the right side of the square.

**You will follow the lead of this servant.**

He raised a gauntlet to indicate Gordo Goldeaxe,

who swooped low on the obsidian dragon he now rode.

**You will go to Legrash. Destroy everything en route, and all who get in your way.**

An eerily quiet cheer went up from the crowd; it sounded like the rustling shrouds of a horde of tortured ghosts.

In anticipation of the dark god's next command, Gape Teethgrit brought the second dragon to ground.

Vanquish addressed the group on his left.

**You others will march for Spittle: every death you cause on the way will drape your immortal soul like a medal. Go now: all will fall! ALL WILL FALL.**

As the former citizens of Dullitch turned and headed for the gates, their masters riding the skies above them, a series of black clouds bubbled over the land.

Vanquish glanced down at the bedraggled rabble who lingered in the centre of the square.

**The rest of you shall remain with me. Guard the harbours . . . and the gates. No one leaves.**

Vanquish turned and marched back towards the palace, his red eyes glowing in the moonlight.

Summoning one of the possessed that staggered along in his wake, he made an indicative sweep of the palace with his hand.

**Amass a selection of my finest souls here. They may enter the palace and watch over me, but I am not to be disturbed. I need time to contemplate and to search the land . . . When I have discovered the location of my**

imprisoned body, I will be able to cast off this pathetic human shell. Then all of Illmoor will fall beneath my wrath.

The enchanted citizen bowed his head.

'Yes, master,' it mouthed.

Effigy and Obegarde had spent a pleasant if somewhat slanted night at Spittle Tower. The beds were comfortable enough, but both of them had woken up on the floor. This morning, following a carefully juggled breakfast, they were ready to face a new raft of challenges.

'Are you sure Jimmy will be able to find those two warriors?' Effigy whispered to Obegarde as they followed Earl Visceral and a troupe of soldiers through the Spittle Tower Gardens. 'I mean, he's not exactly—'

'From what I know of Jimmy,' Obegarde interrupted, 'he'll find them all right. He was working as a scout during the Rat Catastrophe, and *he* was the one who found Groan and Gordo and managed to enlist the pair of them. He's more than capable, Effigy. You really should give him more credit.'

'I suppose so; it's just that he tends to antagonize people; he's not much of a fighter; and I'd hate it if he got hurt or killed because—'

'Jimmy's as quick as a cat, and twice as lucky. He survived the Yowler, and a lot more since. Besides, Visceral's given him the fastest horse in the city! I

seriously doubt he'll run into anything he can't handle.'

'Well, I hope to the gods you're right . . .'

'If I may interrupt, gentlemen, we're nearly there.'

Earl Visceral led the group to the door of a large cottage in the grounds of his tower.

'This is the place where most matters of great importance are usually discussed,' he said, as one of his soldiers unlocked the front door. 'We tend not to put important or regal visitors through the endurance test the tower tends to be . . .'

'It was all right for us, I notice,' Obegarde whispered to Effigy, who made every effort to avoid laughing.

'In here,' Earl Visceral continued, leading the way into the cottage's expansive meeting room. 'I'm told our guests will be with us shortly?'

The page beside him nodded. 'We have confirmations via ravensage: within the hour.'

'Good, good! Obegarde, do take a seat. Effigy, you should definitely sit near the top of the table: your account of things will be vital.'

The freedom fighter nodded, and took the proffered seat.

'Who's coming again?' Obegarde wanted to know.

'Well,' Earl Visceral began, 'as I said before, we can expect the support of Viceroy Funk, Lord of Beanstalk, and Baron Muttknuckles of Sneeze – mainly because their towns would be swept through en route to ours.

The big question hangs over Legrash. I have been assured that Prince Blood is coming to the table, but getting him to commit his army to any kind of enterprise will be tricky.'

'Why?' Effigy snapped. 'Vanquish is as likely to head for Legrash as he is for Spittle!'

'Indeed – yet Blood can be very difficult about these things. His ravensage reply betrayed little *real* concern, and he's inevitably the last to contribute *anything* to a national cause.'

'Because he's too wrapped up in his own affairs?' asked Effigy.

Visceral shrugged. 'Perhaps he believes that Legrash's defences can withstand any invaders.'

'But he's labouring under a misapprehension. Vanquish would annihilate Legrash in a heartbeat!'

'*I* know that, and *you* know that,' said the earl, with a sigh. 'Our job is to convince *him* of the imminent threat Vanquish poses to the whole of Illmoor.'


The horse thundered across the landscape like a rogue missile, taking every twist and turn as if it was capable of predicting the land.

Jimmy dug in his heels several times, then brought the animal screeching to a halt beside two beggars on the Mavokhan Road.

'I'm on royal business,' he said, producing two crowns from his pack and holding them in plain sight,

'and I'm looking for two men: one a barbarian, the other cloaked.'

The beggars shared a glance before one stepped forward slightly.

'I seen two men,' he said. 'One was definitely a barbarian.'

'And the other?'

'Wore a big cloak – jus' like you said.'

Jimmy smiled humourlessly.

'What colour?'

'Eh?'

'What colour was the man's cloak?'

'Oh, it were . . . red . . .'

'That's wrong.'

'. . . to start with, it were red,' said the second beggar, sensing that his friend had lost the edge. 'Then it changed to black, depending on how you looked at it.'

'I see,' said Jimmy, knowingly. 'It didn't go through any shades of green, then?'

'Funny you should say that,' the first beggar began, but he didn't get a chance to say anything else: the horse was already a speck in the middle distance.

Jimmy's next two stops were equally disappointing: an old lady with a long, warty nose swore blind she'd seen the duo leaving Plunge, while a portly bartender at an inn just north of Fogrise reckoned he'd seen both men heading towards Chudderford. Unfortunately, neither of them had picked green for the cloak, leaving Jimmy right back where he started.

The horse slowed to a trot as he progressed through the Mountains of Mavokhan. Jimmy rubbed his chin, thoughtfully. He *didn't* want to enter Grinswood Forest, that was for sure – but what choice did he have? If the pair had genuinely continued to head west, they could only *be* in one place, and that meant— Jimmy looked up, suddenly. A traveller was approaching, mounted on horseback.

He carefully urged his own horse onward.

'Well met,' came a shout, when he was just a few metres away from the rider.

'And you,' Jimmy called back. 'I am looking for two men who were said to be on this path: have you seen anyone?'

The man reined in his horse. He was middle-aged, and somewhat vacant-looking.

'Either of your two men an elf?'

Jimmy hesitated. 'No,' he said, with a sigh. 'Neither is an elf, as far as I know.'

'Well, the chap I passed was wearing a green hood, and I usually associate that with the forest-folk.'

'It could be him I'm after!' Jimmy confirmed, quickly producing a crown and tossing it to the traveller, who caught it immediately. 'Was he travelling with a barbarian?'

'Nope; he was on his own,' the rider muttered. 'But I

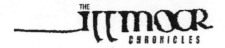

wouldn't bother looking for him – he's dead.'

Jimmy's face fell.

'By your hand?' he wondered aloud.

'I'm no murderer,' said the man. 'But the man you seek was heading into Cambleton Valley, on the western beard of Grinswood. It's a place folk don't return from – werewolf country.'

Jimmy thought for a moment, then shrugged.

'The man I seek is a troll-killer,' he said. 'There's a chance I can still find him alive.'

The rider smiled, sullenly.

'You go in there,' he said, pointing behind him, 'and you'll find nothing but your end.'

He sighed and urged his horse onward, calling back: 'Good luck. You'll need it!'

Jimmy ignored him, and focussed his concentration on the wood. It wasn't exactly a big deal, he told himself. After all, his friend and fellow thief, Grab Dafisful, had ventured into Grinswood a few years back, and *he* had come out alive.

The wood *did* look menacing, but they *all* did, until you went in a little way . . . then it usually turned out to be a walk in the park.

Jimmy swallowed a few times, and dug in his heels. The horse moved forward, and plunged into the wood.

# Three

Following Diek's encounter with the troglodyte war-band, Burnie had managed to persuade Slythi to change direction and march for Spittle. The troglodyte king wasn't exactly happy about the situation, but even he had relented at the thought of a legendary hero like Groan ending up in a small box.

Groan, for his part, had been silent since the memory of Gordo had resurfaced. And Burnie's suggestion that he'd lost his physical body to Vanquish hadn't helped matters.

'I'm sure you didn't kill your friend,' said Diek, quietly wondering if he could leave the box with the troglodytes and sneak back home. He was sure his

parents would be pleased to see him . . . if they were still alive. 'I mean, your memory is still fuzzy from the possession, or whatever it was . . . you don't actually *know* you hurt him, do you? It's all guesswork, isn't it?'

No sound came from the box.

'I'd give him time to reflect on things,' said Burnie, who'd dropped back in order to give Diek some warm furs to wear. 'After all, it really isn't his fault: according to my king, Vanquish is a *god* – and you can't fight a god. At least, not on your own.'

'I wasn' on me own,' came the voice, suddenly. 'I was wiv Gordo 'n' Gape.'

'Yes, but—'

'I wonder what 'appened to Gape. I don' 'member anyfing 'bout 'im.'

'Well, he probably got away, then,' Diek said, reassuringly.

Burnie cast a sideways glance at the boy.

'I don't mean to keep on,' he said, doubtfully. 'But are you *really* Diek Wustapha?'

'Yes.'

'And you've actually been trapped in another plane since the Rat Catastrophe, all those years back?'

'Yes.'

'Wow. So you've been in the dark place ever since?'

'Yeah,' said Diek, touching his face self-consciously. 'I just hope my mum and dad are still . . . around.'

'Well—'

'*I* 'ope Gordo's still 'round,' Groan interrupted. ''Sme best mate.'

The pair walked in silence for a time, before Burnie noticed that the warband had shuffled to a halt.

'What's the problem?' he called, hurrying up to Slythi.

The king drove his sword into the stout trunk of a nearby tree.

'Edge jungle,' he yapped. 'Big bunoak: see all.'

Burnie gazed up at the immense tree, as a troglodyte warrior scampered up it like a giant squirrel (albeit a green squirrel . . . covered in snot). He was gone for ten minutes.

'What there?' Slythi barked. 'See you? What there?'

'Mishmash,' said the returning troglodyte, shaking its warty head. 'Mishmash biiiiig.'

Diek, who'd caught up and was trying to make sense of the conversation, looked to Burnie.

'We've hit the Gleaming Mountains,' said the troglodyte councillor.

'Is that good?'

'Not really, just means it's all uphill from here.'

'Can't we go *round* them?'

Burnie shook his head. 'Nope. Going round west would set us back *days* and going round east would take us too close to Dullitch – which would be especially dangerous since we don't know what's going on there, right now. We'll have to go through the mountains. Is that all right with you, Slythi?'

The troglodyte king removed his sword from the tree and nodded.

'Mishmash climb,' he muttered. 'Mishmash hard climb.'

A line of carriages rattled through the grounds of Spittle Tower. One had already arrived at the little cottage, disgorging Viceroy Funk and several of his lackeys. Another carriage, several back, had produced two Phlegmian assistants who were struggling valiantly to entice their royal steward out of his transport.

'No! I'm not coming out,' snapped a high-pitched and rather grating voice. 'I look terrible.'

'You don't, sir. Honestly!' said one of the pages, who was supporting a magnificent cushion between his hands.

'I do! And I don't *want* the cushion. I want to stay on the spike. Not *this* spike, though – it's an absolute disgrace . . .'

'But, sir . . .'

'Oh, all right! Just get on with it, would you!'

Loogie Lambontroff was giving his servants hell. The two men gingerly reached into the carriage before one emerged with what appeared to be a very long lance. There was a human head impaled on the top of it.

'I didn't ask for the blue spike,' it moaned. 'I wanted the red spike, with the gold lace . . . it makes me look younger.'

'Really, sir, I do think—'

'Well *don't*! You don't know what it's like to be a *head*.'

'No I don't, sir, but—'

'Then shut up.'

'Yes, sir.'

'Are you shutting up?'

'Yes, sir.'

'Good. Who's holding me?'

'Mr Theoff, sir.'

'Is he holding me upright? Everything looks a bit . . . slanted.'

Mr Theoff checked himself, and quickly straightened the lance.

'I'm s-sorry, sir,' said his colleague. 'Mr Theoff is quite new to all this.'

'Then why aren't YOU holding me?'

'Er . . . my hands are still sore from the branding, sir.'

Loogie rolled his eyes. 'Yeah well, you deserved *that* . . .'

'I know, sir.'

'Saying that we should get *ahead* of the other carriages was nothing short of bloody insensitive.'

'Yes, sir. I AM sorry, sir.'

'Right, well . . . Can we go in, do you think?'

'Of course, sir! Mr Theoff – on the double!'

The lance-wielder marched smartly towards the cottage, where Earl Visceral was waiting to meet and greet his special guests.

'Steward Lambontroff!' he declared. 'What an honour! Thank you *so* much for coming . . .'

'Whatever – just let me get inside. I thought I could hear an eagle just now . . .'

'Oh . . . we have a few flying wild around the grounds.'

'Yeah, well I'm feeling a bit exposed here, and if I lose an eye on top of everything else, I'm not going to be up to much, am I?'

Visceral nodded and stepped aside so that Lambontroff's entourage could carry him in. Unfortunately, the door had swung shut.

'Arghgh!'

'I'm so sorry, sir!'

'What am I now, a bloody battering ram?'

The second page hurried forward and opened the door. Mr Theoff carefully proceded inside, the lance held out before him, while Earl Visceral did his best to keep a straight face.

Viceroy Funk had also arrived. A small and decidedly ugly little man with prominent teeth and wild blond hair, he sidled up to the earl, coughing loudly.

Visceral smiled at him. 'Welcome, Viceroy.'

'Eh?'

'I said "Welcome".'

'You can see me?'

'What?'

'Can you actually see me?'

'Of course.'

'But I'm wearing my magic bracelet!'

'Really? Well, I'm very sorry—'

'Can you see *all* of me?'

Visceral looked the viceroy up and down. 'What there *is* to see, yes.'

'How many fingers am I holding up?'

'Twelve.'

'What about now?'

'Six.'

Funk glared down at his wrist and began to slap the band of gold that was fastened to it.

'Damn Muttknuckles and his dodgy gear. I paid five hundred crowns for this! No wonder the wretch hasn't turned up . . .'

'Yes, well, there are far more important things to discuss, so if you'd just move inside . . .'

Visceral waited for the viceroy to comply, then turned his attention to the coach he had been waiting for: the Legrasian flag flew from it in every direction, large and resplendent.

It didn't surprise Visceral that the door was opened from inside, or that Prince Blood didn't wait for a servant before jumping down and heading for the cottage. The prince was all about strength and pride . . . and he looked every inch the noble.

'Before you ask, I *do* have a very good reason for calling you here,' Visceral began.

'I don't want *reasons*,' Blood muttered, walking past the earl and into the cottage, 'I want evidence. Only then will you have the backing of Legrash.'

Earl Visceral shook his head, sadly . . . and followed the lords inside.

# Four

It would be fair to say that Jimmy Quickstint knew there was something wrong with Charney the second he laid eyes on it. The town consisted of ten cottages, all huddled together . . . and there wasn't a single light visible. The entire place was shrouded in darkness; even the light of the full moon failed to illuminate it.

Jimmy carefully urged his horse down into the valley . . . and then tugged sharply on the reins: a blood-curdling howl had split the silence of the night.

Jimmy gulped. Even as he watched the town, he felt instinctively that something was watching him.

The second howl was louder, but it was also too close for comfort – Jimmy slapped his horse on the flank and

galloped headlong through the town, screaming encouragement at the horse when he realized that at least one wolf was now tracking him.

Head down, he clung on to the reins for dear life, darting glances left and right as several wolves appeared and began to keep pace with the horse.

Jimmy's eyes filled with tears as the wind whipped at his face. The horse was picking up speed, leaving the town far behind, but still the wolves were almost upon them.

The valley road, which was nothing more than a winding dirt track, caused the horse plenty of effort on the ravine bends. The wolves, on the other hand, had no such problems . . . and, seizing the initiative, one leaped.

Jimmy twisted in the saddle to avoid the beast, but failed to move in time: it cannoned into him and the two of them crashed to the ground. The horse bolted.

Jimmy wriggled out from under the beast, momentarily surprised that it let him go so easily. Then he saw why: several of the creatures had gathered around him, circling and sizing up their prey. They obviously intended to have some fun before they fed.

'I'm armed,' Jimmy said, cursing the nervous squeak in his voice. He slid a long knife from the arm of his jerkin. 'You'd do well to stay back.'

The wolves were obviously used to working together: the first feigned a leap – which Jimmy immediately ducked – before the second leaped over it in order to catch him on the ground.

An axe-head cut the beast in two.

Jimmy rolled on to his back, shielding his face from the shower of blood that splashed over him.

Grid Thungus stepped on to the path, as casually as if he'd been out for an afternoon stroll. He stepped over Jimmy Quickstint and swung the great axe a second time, sending the wolves scrambling backwards.

'Dangerous place for a man to wander,' he growled. 'You've either got too much confidence, a death-wish, or both.'

The barbarian produced what looked like a butcher's knife from his belt-pouch and pitched it at the pack, downing a second wolf. The others shrank back into the undergrowth.

'Up with you,' Thungus snapped. 'And if I need to tell you to get the hell out of here, you've lived too long already.'

'Wait!' Jimmy cried, struggling to his feet and hurrying after the barbarian. 'I think you might be the man I'm looking for!'

Thungus snorted. 'I doubt it. People don't *look* for me – they tend to *avoid* me.'

'But are you not Grid Thungus?'

The barbarian stopped dead, and turned very slowly to face his pursuer. 'I am. What of it?'

'You travel with a man called Moltenoak?'

Thungus narrowed his eyes. 'I may do. Who's asking?'

'Earl Visceral.'

'HIM? Why? We did a job, he paid us, we left. What more is there to say?'

'You killed all those trolls, right?'

'We . . . helped out, certainly.'

'Exactly.' Jimmy nodded, catching his breath. 'Do you think you could kill a dragon?'

'A what?' A green-cloaked figure emerged from the edge of the woods, his cape billowing out behind him. He was leading Jimmy's lost horse. 'I'll forget the fact that you said my name aloud – if your question has a story behind it. A dragon, you say?'

'A dragon,' Jimmy repeated, stepping back as the second man, presumably the one called Moltenoak, tethered the horse to a tree and moved to join Thungus on the road. 'A dark god has risen up to claim the capital. It has two obsidian dragons working for it.'

Grid glanced at his companion, whose eyes were glowing red. 'What god has the power to summon dragons to the realm?'

'He's called Vanquish.' Jimmy wiped some sweat from his forehead. 'There's little doubt that he'll take the whole of Illmoor if he isn't stopped. I expect the reward would be . . . huge. In fact, I'd be surprised if money is an object on this sort of quest . . .'

Grid Thungus sniffed. 'How tough is an obsidian dragon?' he asked his companion.

Moltenoak shrugged. 'Harder than a cave dragon, weaker than a frostworm.'

'Could we take one?'

'*I* could, given a bit of luck and the right circumstances.'

'Two?'

'Tricky.' The hooded man regarded Jimmy Quickstint. 'I know Vanquish,' he said, quietly. 'You don't stand a chance.'

It took a few moments for Moltenoak's words to sink in.

'Y-you *know* him?' Jimmy gasped. 'You mean, as in, know *of* him?'

'No, I mean I *know* him . . . and he's about as bad as they get.'

Jimmy shook his head in disbelief; even Grid looked shocked.

'B-but Vanquish is a god; an actual dark *god*. How can you possibly KNOW him? He's . . . from the other side.'

'Only since he became imprisoned.' Moltenoak smiled, and his red eyes suddenly seemed to light up the hood he was wearing. 'Before that, he walked the land. Long, long ago.'

'B-but how can you *know* him?'

This time, it was Thungus who answered. 'My friend is very old,' he said. 'Very, very old.'

Jimmy squinted at Moltenoak: the man appeared to be in his early forties.

'But that's ridiculous! I mean, we're talking hundreds of years, right? Thousands?'

'Oh yes.' Moltenoak yawned. 'But, please, don't go *on* about it . . . I hate being reminded of my age.'

'I'm s-sorry,' Jimmy blurted, trying to wrench his eyes from the man but finding himself unable to do so. 'E-earl Visceral is trying to form an alliance with the other lor—'

'Should we really get involved in this?' Thungus grumbled, eyeing his companion doubtfully. 'I mean, it's not our problem, is it? Don't get me wrong; I can take on anything, me. But it sounds like a lot of hassle for uncertain pay . . .'

Moltenoak turned to him, a smile still playing on his lips.

'If Vanquish has truly broken from his eternal prison, no corner of the land will be safe from him,' he said.

'W-what about Trod?'

'Heathen Trod?'

'Yeah – we could always get a ship and—'

'Have you ever *been* to Trod, Thungus?'

Grid sniffed, shook his head. 'Nope.'

'Right, then. Let's go and have a talk with the earl, shall we?'

'I've only got one horse,' Jimmy admitted. 'I doubt all three of us could get on. Are there any other towns in this part of Grinswood?'

Moltenoak shook his head. 'None, but a horse isn't necessary. We will . . . make our own way to Spittle.'

'Yeah,' Thungus added. 'Don't worry about us.'

'Eh?' Jimmy glanced from one to the other. 'But it's miles away . . .'

The barbarian shrugged. 'I'll wager we arrive before you,' he muttered.

'You're serious?'

'Deadly.'

'Whatever you say!' Jimmy turned and hurried over to his horse. 'I guess I'll see you in Spittle, then . . .'

'Aye,' Thungus grinned. 'That you will.'

The two men watched as Jimmy charged the horse through the wood.

After a few seconds, Thungus turned to his companion. 'Shall we go?'

'Not yet,' said Moltenoak, wearily. 'Let's give him a head start, at least . . .'

'If we must,' Thungus growled.

'Before we leave, I want to . . . take a look at the situation for myself.'

He moved over to a nearby tree and placed his hand firmly on the trunk. The wood reacted almost immediately, melting around his touch as if he'd plunged his hand into water.

Grid Thungus looked on in amazement; he'd seen the trick a few times now, but it never ceased to astonish him.

Moltenoak withdrew his hand from the tree; then he drew back his hood and plunged his head inside it. The wood solidified around his neck.

Several seconds passed, but the silence was soon interrupted.

There was a low rumble, and the tree began to creak. This went on for no more than a few seconds; then the ground started to shake beneath them. The mini-quake continued unabated for a time, before seeming to move off into the distance.

Silence returned.

'Just because I watch this stuff, doesn't mean I'm impressed by it,' Thungus lied, rubbing his beard distractedly. He always felt the need to carry on talking with Moltenoak during these 'events', even though it was quite obvious his words were being lost. 'Another few minutes, I expect,' he said, pointlessly, watching his companion with a careful eye. 'No more, certainly. Pretty amazing, I suppose . . . considering the distance you manage to cover. Five, four, three, two, two and a half . . .'

Sure enough, the distant rumble became audible again a minute or two later. It grew steadily as the forest ground joined in, causing Thungus to grab for a nearby branch in order to keep his stance.

The tree swirled again, and Moltenoak withdrew from it. Stepping back, the hooded man closed his eyes and muttered something under his breath.

'Well?' Thungus prompted him. 'What's happening?' Moltenoak sighed.

'Unusual,' he said. 'My tree-eye failed to penetrate the capital. Vanquish must have grown very powerful indeed.'

'You didn't see *anything*?' Thungus shook his head. 'That's bad, especially if—'

'I didn't say I saw *nothing*. I just said that I couldn't see inside the capital. What I did see was two armies . . .'

'Two?'

'Yes; both led by dragon-riders. One was heading in the direction of Spittle. The other was going north-west, to Legrash if I'm any judge.'

'These armies . . .' Thungus grimaced. 'Are they . . . undead?'

'More like the walking possessed,' Moltenoak hazarded. 'Either way, the situation is worse than suspected. Now let's get moving – we've given the boy enough of a lead to at least make it an interesting race . . .'

# Five

'Far eye! Far eye!'

Diek couldn't tell *what* was going on. The troglodyte warband had been negotiating the mountain rise when two of the unit scouts had come charging back to speak with Slythi. Now, even Burnie looked worried.

'Wha's goin' on?' Groan's voice boomed.

'I don't know,' Diek admitted.

'Far eye!' Slythi was croaking. 'Far eye! Far eye!'

A rather fat troglodyte hurried up to the king, unhooking a tied pack that was attached to his spines. He rummaged around inside, produced a telescopic device and handed it to the king. Slythi made a gesture to Burnie and the two troglodytes dashed off to join the scouts, who had vanished soon after their inexplicable whisperings.

At the mountain edge, Burnie waited for the king to finish looking through the telescope before taking the device and holding it up to his own gloopy eye.

He was silent for some time. Then both he and the king dashed back to join the warband.

'What is it?' Diek asked, rushing over to Burnie at the first opportunity. 'What's happened?'

The little troglodyte rubbed his emerald forehead.

'There's an army of zombies on the move,' he said. 'Judging by the sheer number, they're from Dullitch.'

'Where are they heading?'

'North. Maybe for Phlegm, or Spittle. There's a dragon flying over them . . . with a rider, I think.'

Diek swallowed a few times. 'This is all very bad, isn't it?'

'As bad as it *can* be.'

'What do we do?'

Burnie sighed. 'We need to get ahead of 'em, somehow. They're not moving *that* fast, so maybe—'

'Burnie! Look!'

Diek's face had gone very pale, and his jaw had dropped.

Burnie spun around, as the rest of the troglodytes rushed over to the opposite edge of the mountain. There was another dragon flapping through the sky . . . and this one was heading straight for them. Burnie

quickly produced the telescope and put it to his eye: a sizeable army was marching up the mountain path, far beneath the beast.

'Run!' Burnie screamed. 'Everybody. *Ruuuunn!*'

'Fight!' Slythi croaked, stopping the warband dead in its tracks. 'Fight we; fight we!'

'Are you crazy?' the little troglodyte screamed. 'We can't fight a dragon! We'll die; we'll all die!'

'Whichways, all die!' Slythi yelled back. 'Whichways, whichways! Arm us! Arm us! Fight we! Fight we!'

As every troglodyte warrior brandished a flail, the dragon began to swoop.

Burnie cast a significant glance at Diek . . . and the two of them took to their feet.


'The defences at Legrash will hold—'

'They will NOT hold against a pair of obsidian dragons and a dark god – honestly, Blood, just *listen* to yourself!'

The argument in the cottage had been raging for several hours. Effigy had opened the meeting with a lengthy (and impressive, Obegarde thought) summary of the events surrounding the fall of Dullitch, but so far, Prince Blood had his head in the sand. If the Legrash noble really *did* believe his city could withstand an attack of the suggested magnitude, Obegarde concluded that he was either completely misguided or irreparably stupid.

'I've put Phlegm on high alert,' said Loogie Lambontroff, who'd been placed on a cushion in the centre of the table. 'After all, we *are* quite near to the capital . . . and I'm not taking any chances. Besides, if the king really *is* lost to us, I need to start thinking about the future of Phlegm.'

'Well said,' Viceroy Funk agreed. 'Beanstalk is a bit further away from the immediate danger zone, but I've got guards on the walls and—'

'How many men do you have, exactly?' Visceral interrupted. 'I mean, are we talking hundreds or thousands here?'

Funk hesitated, his eyes flicking from lord to lord. 'Er . . . I have about a hundred armed guards in Beanstalk,' he admitted.

'And you, Steward?'

'I have about a hundred, give or take.'

'These numbers are not enough!' Visceral cried. 'I myself can muster no more than a few hundred troops.' He turned imploringly to the prince. 'Surely you will help us, Blood? You *must* realize that Vanquish will come for Legrash on a whim – you are NOT safe from him.'

'Possibly . . .' Prince Blood stared down furious glares from Effigy and Obegarde before returning his attention to the other lords. 'However, giving you the thousand or so troops at my disposal merely to watch you run them into dragonfire is *not* my idea of warfare. Would you really have an army, even one so vast, attack

such living nightmares with sticks, stones, swords and pikes? It's pathetic, man – it's almost entirely futile . . .'

'Then what do YOU suggest, your Majesty?' Effigy cut in, when he could hold himself back no longer. 'That we all gather together in Legrash and hide behind the MIGHTY WALLS THAT CAN WITHSTAND ANY AND ALL ATTACKS? I don't think so . . .'

'Hear, hear,' Obegarde muttered.

'On the contrary – I think we should call upon the Trodlings to aid us.'

A deathly silence settled over the room, as various horrified expressions met those across the table.

'You can't be serious,' Visceral snapped. 'You would ally yourself with the enemy to defeat a problem on our own soil?'

Prince Blood sighed. 'We know nothing of Trod, save what is told to us by the few who return from the place. We *do* know they are heathens . . . but the fact—'

'This fight is *ours*,' Viceroy Funk said, sharply. 'We don't want to solicit the help of an unknown and untested foe, merely to have them invade Illmoor off the back of any victory, however unlikely, that we may secure over the fell beast who now walks our land.'

'May I remind you that Trod has never attacked the shores of Illmoor—'

'. . . as we have never attacked the shores of Trod,' Visceral finished. 'It does not mean we are allied: what it means is that we are totally alien to each other. Such an alliance is, to my mind, out of the question.'

Viceroy Funk nodded. 'I agree.'

'I hate to say it,' Effigy added, 'but, speaking as a free citizen of Dullitch, I have to concede the point myself. A foreign and unknown land should be our very last resort – such a request may well throw up more problems than it solves.'

Visceral nodded gravely. 'Will you not assist us by lending your army?' he asked the prince, his voice now near to desperation. 'Please?'

Prince Blood took a deep breath.

'I'm afraid not,' he said – and rose to his feet.

The dragon flew out of the sky like a dart, Gordo Goldeaxe screaming short commands from its back. The beast spewed a gout of flame across the mountain top, burning three troglodytes where they stood and causing a rush of panic among the others. Several of the warriors leaped into the air, flailing wildly with their swords, but the dragon was way beyond their reach.

Slythi had retreated to the back of the group. Untying a spear from his own pack and raising it above his head, he began to run towards the dragon as it came in for its second sweep. Two more troglodytes erupted in flames on the new pass, but Slythi had managed to avoid the fire. He took three final, giant leaps and flung the spear with all his might: it lodged in the dragon's stomach,

causing the beast to falter slightly as it rose back into the air.

'Spear want!' the king screamed at his remaining men. 'Spear want!'

A small troglodyte armourer hurried up to him and thrust a new spear into his claw-like hand.

Slythi took a few steps back, and waited for the dragon to return. The great creature wheeled in the air, the spear still lodged in its gut, and dived again.

This time, the jet of flame consumed six troglodytes, causing the others to scream in terror and frustration.

Slythi, on the other hand, wasn't having any of it. He flung the second spear, which again lodged in the dragon's gut, about twenty centimetres from the first. This time, the great beast cried out.

Sensing the danger posed by the troglodyte king, Gordo dived from the dragon's back and rolled as he landed, drawing the immense battleaxe from its shoulder strap as he reached his feet.

Slythi growled, and the two opponents circled each other warily.

'Sword want!' the troglodyte king screamed, throwing down his flail. 'Now! Sword want!'

He caught the first blade that was thrown to him, then had to dodge the other two.

Gordo marched determinedly forward, prepared to take on both the king and the pair of troglodyte soldiers who had taken positions beside him.

The dragon, still wheeling far above, dived yet again, driving the remaining troops towards the army of possessed men that was rising up the mountainside.

Chaos reigned.

Further along the rocky path that wound down the far side of the mountain, Diek and Burnie were hurrying to escape the explosive conflict behind them.

'Th-they don't stand a chance!' Diek cried, leaping over rocks and rogue bushes while carefully clasping the box in both hands.

'Slythi's a fool!' Burnie replied. 'He should have ordered a retreat! I told him to—'

'Wha's 'appenin'?' said Groan's voice. 'All I can 'ear is screamin'!'

'That's all there *is* to hear,' Diek replied, narrowly avoiding the treacherous edge of the path he was on.

'We were attacked by an obsidian dragon,' Burnie croaked. 'Now we're trying to escape.'

'Dragons 're 'ard.'

'We know that!' Burnie blurted. 'That's why we're running away.'

'Besides, it's leading an army of zombies,' managed Diek, tucking the box under his arm as he ran.

'Did you see the dwarf?' Burnie asked.

'Dwarf? Where?'

'It was riding the dragon.'

'Really?'

'Yeah; fiery beard and a mean-looking axe strapped behind it.'

'I don't like dwarfs,' Diek snapped. He didn't know quite why he said it, but he realized, in voicing the opinion, that it was true.

'Tha' sounds like Gordo,' Groan boomed. 'Bu' he wouldn' side wiv no dragon.'

'Maybe he had *his* body taken, too,' Burnie muttered. 'Still, look on the bright side – at least you didn't kill him . . .'

'Yeah,' the barbarian mumbled. 'I s'pose so.'

Behind and above them, the battle on the mountaintop raged on.

The dragon, having totally eviscerated the remaining troglodytes, had landed on the rise. Two soulless scouts, the first of their army to reach the mountaintop, hurried over to the beast and carefully removed the spears from its side. The resulting wounds healed up before the zombies had even cast the spears aside.

The dragon turned towards the dwarf and the troglodyte king, its great yellow eyes watching the unfolding duel with intent curiosity.

Gordo jumped to his left, avoiding a flail-lunge, and cleanly decapitated the first of the troglodyte king's bodyguard.

The second caused him more of a problem, glancing two mighty blows off his iron helm before he managed to cleave the warrior in two.

Gordo didn't get a moment to reflect on the kill before Slythi barrelled into him, literally peppering the dwarf with sword strikes. Gordo blocked the first, but then took two nasty arm-wounds before he managed to dive aside and bring up his battleaxe in a defensive block.

There was a furious clash of steel, but the king was relentless. His next three attacks caused Gordo to suffer gashes to the face and both legs. Eventually, the dwarf turned and retreated, hurrying towards the sanctuary of the crouched dragon.

Slythi made to pursue him, then stopped, a look of terrible certainty on his scaly face.

The dragon had unfolded, its wing-spread an awesome sight on the great mountaintop.

'Coward are!' Slythi taunted the dwarf, as he saw Gordo climb the monster's side. 'Coward are! Coward are!'

Now astride the beast once again, Gordo urged it forward, its giant nostrils flaring.

King Slythi recognized the danger, and turned to run. He got about twenty paces before the hellfires rolled over him, reducing the troglodyte king to ash.

# Six

'I'm sorry, gentlemen,' Prince Blood finished, moving towards the cottage door, 'but I'm not willing to send my men to their almost certain death without first exploring *every* avenue open to consideration. I wish you all the best of luck defeating this evil, but for now I must adjourn.'

To the accompaniment of a series of vengeful mutterings, Blood made his way to the door and wrenched it open, just as an out-of-breath guard fell against the frame.

'Visitors, my lords!' he managed. 'They say it's urgent business!'

'No visitors today,' Visceral snapped. 'They can

see me at the weekly forum, if it's a matter of publi—'

'Lady Vanya said I should bring them both straight here, my lords! They arrived in the courtyard while she was helping to groom the horses.'

Earl Visceral rubbed his tired eyes. 'Very well,' he said. 'Send them in.'

The guard moved aside, admitting the imposing form of Grid Thungus and his cloaked companion.

'What's this?' asked Blood. 'Some sort of dance troupe?'

Grid Thungus muttered something under his breath and shoved the prince backwards, causing him to collapse on to a chair.

'How *DARE* you!' Blood screamed. 'Do you have any idea who—'

'Prince Viktar Blood,' Moltenoak stated. 'Son of Etley Blood, grandson of Irmington Blood, great-grandson of Torrider Blood . . . and arguably the most spineless member of the entire line. You run Legrash – when it suits you – and a more hideous den of depraved villainy I've seldom seen. You have no children, which really grates on your nerves, as the only thing that has ever mattered to you is passing on the crumbled wreckage of a throne you yourself inherited at the age of sixteen. Any questions?'

The room had become suddenly very quiet. A group of guards had gathered outside the door as a result of

the commotion, but none of them appeared keen to enter the building.

'Do you mind if *I* ask who *you* are?' said Loogie Lambontroff, oblivious of the fact that Earl Visceral was attempting to get his attention with a series of nods and silently mouthed indications.

'My name is Moltenoak,' said the hooded man, drawing level with the table and taking an empty seat beside it. 'My companion is the fabled warrior known as Grid Thungus. We are here to assist your ... current dilemma.'

Effigy Spatula smiled. 'Jimmy found you, then?' he said, his face alight with glee.

'He did,' Moltenoak confirmed, casting a sideways glance at his companion. 'But I think he'll be a while yet ... we knew a shortcut here.'

'What can you do?' Obegarde said. 'I mean, how much do you actually *know*?'

'We know that Vanquish has taken the city of Dullitch, and that he has two dragons working for hi—'

'Do you know that Vanquish is a dark god?' Effigy interrupted. 'And that he has taken the body of Groan Teethgrit as his vessel?'

'Groan Teethgrit?' Thungus exclaimed. 'I'm sorry to hear such news – Groan was a good friend of mine.'

Prince Blood, who had until now been silently fuming, could contain himself no longer.

'You stride in here, as if you are royalty yourself!' he

growled at Moltenoak. 'And yet what are *you* going to do against a pair of dragons? Not much, I'll wager!'

Moltenoak turned to him, and nodded.

'You're absolutely right, your Majesty. I'm not going to do anything against two dragons. *My* time is best invested in the reclaiming of Dullitch. Therefore, I will fight Vanquish and attempt to take the city back. My friend here will help you with the dragons. He has some experience with them.'

All eyes flicked from Moltenoak to Thungus, and back again.

'You're going to take on a dark god?' Prince Blood sneered. 'Who exactly *are* you?'

Moltenoak placed both hands flat on the tabletop.

'I have told you my name,' he began. 'I am . . . very old – and quite powerful in many ways. Do not question my word or think to second-guess me in any way, and I will do my best to see you through this situation. Understand that I do this thing not for money or reward, but because I know the foe you face of old . . . and I utterly despise him. Now – before I begin, does anyone wish to challenge me?'

The room suddenly contained a large selection of shocked and, in most cases, preoccupied expressions.

'Very good. First of all, I must tell you that even now Vanquish scours the land in search of his true body— no, no questions please – just know that he will not find it . . . and that I am already in the process of blocking his

powerful sight. My own special talents tell me that he removed the souls of three warriors and many thousands of unfortunate citizens who now follow his word, their bodies commanded by his own cursed pool of hive-minds. Of the warriors – as you point out – Groan Teethgrit is currently serving as Vanquish's own temporary vessel. The others – Groan's barbarian brother and the dwarf, Gordo Goldeaxe – have also been utilized and are leading his two black hordes, accompanied by the dragons you're all rightly worried about.'

Effigy looked at Moltenoak with a sudden, incredible respect. Even Obegarde looked shocked. The lords ranged around the table began to mutter among themselves, but Moltenoak spoke again, forcing them into silence.

'Firstly, I shall attack Vanquish at his base in Dullitch Palace. While I am occupied thus, I will require a small group of fighters to perform a very delicate mission for me.'

'I'll gladly help!' Effigy shouted, rising from his seat.

'Count me in,' Obegarde added. 'And I'm sure Jimmy will be on board: he knows the city better than anyone. What is it you want us to do?'

Moltenoak appeared to study the vampire, but when he spoke it soon became clear that his words were directed at his own companion.

'Coming and going between many lands as I do,

I am not *greatly* familiar with Illmoor's current mythology. However, I am given to believe that Groan Teethgrit, Gape Teethgrit and Gordo Goldeaxe are among the most legendary heroes of this age ... is that correct?'

'I don't know Gape that well, Molten,' Thungus growled. 'But Groan and Gordo 'ave taken on plenty of things I wouldn't touch in a million years – and won. They were a mighty pair, the talking point of just about every inn from here to Shadewell.'

Moltenoak widened his grin and turned back to Effigy and Obegarde.

'Then your cause cannot afford to lose them to the enemy without a fight. Therefore, Effigy, Obegarde and their redoubtable friend will travel with me to Dullitch and locate the soul-carriers that contain the three spirits. Break them open and the souls will quickly return to their original hosts.'

Effigy glanced at Obegarde, and the pair of them nodded.

'You may be able to do the same for the citizens of Dullitch,' Moltenoak continued, 'but I'm guessing that Vanquish will have their wretched containers moving along with his army. Nevertheless, you should *all* look out for these receptacles as potential targets. Break them ... and those who bear arms against you *will* regain their senses.'

'Wait just a second.' Prince Blood struggled to

his feet. Placing both hands flat on the tabletop, he leaned across to the hooded man and said: 'Now, I've listened patiently to your little speech and I'd like to have a few words myself. I don't know exactly *who* you think you are . . . but *we* give the orders around here and—'

Moltenoak looked up suddenly and snatched Prince Blood by the throat, yanking his head down so they were face to face. The prince stared in terror at the two pinpoints of screaming energy that Moltenoak's eyes had become.

'You will do exactly what is asked of you,' he growled, in a voice like thunder, 'and you shall keep your kingdom. Otherwise, Legrash and the very foundations it once stood upon will be *no more* . . . by my *own* hand.'

He threw the trembling royal aside, and turned to address the group at the table.

'Two armies are on the move, my friends. One is headed here – via Phlegm, no doubt. The other has begun to cross the Gleaming Mountains.'

'Phlegm?' Loogie screeched. 'Oh, that's great, that is! And to think I'd just got the place looking decent . . .'

'The other is presumably heading for Legrash,' said Earl Visceral, giving the prince a significant look. 'Let's hope your legendary defences hold out.'

'What do *you* suggest we do?' Effigy asked Moltenoak, prompting murmurs of agreement and causing every head in the room to turn towards the hooded man.

Moltenoak took a deep breath, and looked to Earl Visceral. 'How many soldiers do you have, exactly?'

'Counting on support from the viceroy here, and Steward Lambontroff, and *assuming* Prince Blood lends aid, we should be able to muster a force of around one thousand five hundred men.' He rose to his feet and began to pace the room. 'Assuming we need to divide in order to conquer these armies, we could send ravensage to Phlegm and Beanstalk, requesting that *ALL* available soldiers should join us, here. Legrash has more troops than the rest of us combined . . . even if Blood *is* insufferably arrogant about the truth of it. I suggest . . .'

There was a sudden intake of breath from Viceroy Funk, who thought he'd guessed the earl's next words. However, he was wrong.

'. . . I suggest that Prince Blood marches his troops out of Legrash, in a move to defend the whole of western Illmoor. That way, we give strong protection to the innocent lives at stake in Legrash itself, as well as those in Beanstalk, Sneeze, Shinbone, Crust, Chudderford and Little Irkesome. I'm sure Viceroy Funk and Baron Muttknuckles – wherever *he* has got to – will assist the battle with their own troops.'

Prince Blood straightened out his long coat, but made no hostile reaction to the comment. 'That said, I shall attempt to put your *ridiculous* plan into action,' he

muttered. 'Though what chance we stand against a dragon is anybody's gu—'

'Grid will go with you,' Moltenoak finished, accompanied by a nod from his companion. 'You will find him a great help in the coming conflict. Allow him to lead your army and you stand at least half a chance: I guarantee that.'

'And *where* do you suggest we make such a stand?' Visceral asked.

Moltenoak smiled.

'Coldstone,' he said.

'Coldstone?' Several of the room's occupants looked confused.

'Coldstone,' Viceroy Funk repeated, as if searching his memory for the name. 'You mean the flat plain of land wedged between the Gleaming Mountains and Little Irkesome?'

'Indeed. It was, after all, the site of Illmoor's first great battle between good and evil – many, many years ago.' He lowered his voice to a barely audible whisper. 'I was . . . on the wrong side, back then.'

There was a pause as everyone present took this in.

'So, in conclusion,' Blood growled, breaking the silence. 'You want me to place my army, along with the armies of Lords Muttknuckles and Funk, into the hands of your barbarian friend—'

'Yes.'

'. . . who is going to lead them to the Coldstone

Plains . . . and into war with an obsidian dragon and a rampaging zombie horde from Dullitch.'

Moltenoak nodded. 'In a nutshell.'

'What of us?' said Earl Visceral, his calculations suddenly revealing an ugly gap in the plan. 'If you are going to Dullitch and your mighty friend is rounding up *all* the armies in the west with Viceroy Funk and Prince Blood, where does that leave myself and Steward Lambontroff?'

Moltenoak sighed.

'It leaves you with your own men, and the promise that myself or my companion will return to assist you just as soon as we are able. I'm afraid I can offer little more in the way of assistance. I'm sorry . . .'

'But that's ridiculous! You're leaving *us* to face the same foe in the north that you're sending an entire *army* to Coldstone to deal with. I mean; what can *we* do? Do you suggest that we stay here and fight over the walls of Spittle?'

'Just listen – listen very carefully.' Moltenoak closed his eyes for a time, and then opened them again. 'I don't want you to confront the second horde and engage them in combat – I want you to travel south and strike at them when they get to Phlegm. It will be what they are least expecting.'

'But—'

'Having got their attention, I then want you to *run*.'

The earl looked momentarily confused. 'Run?' he exclaimed. 'Run where, exactly?'

'To Coldstone,' Effigy said, suddenly reading the hooded man's train of thought, 'where the second conflict will be taking place. Am I right?'

Moltenoak nodded.

'That way,' he said, 'at least you all fight *together*.'

'A good plan,' said Viceroy Funk.

'I think it's the best we've heard,' added Lambontroff, evenly.

'Hear, hear,' said Effigy and Obegarde, in unison.

'I . . . suppose it would be wise,' Visceral finished, but his face betrayed the hopelessness he felt.

As the earl returned to his seat and lowered his head in despair, the guards at the door parted to reveal the breathless form of Jimmy Quickstint.

'I d-don't believe it,' he panted. 'You're here. You two are actually h-h-here.' And with that, he collapsed.


Diek and Burnie hurried down the mountain path, allowing themselves to slow for breath only when they absolutely had to.

'W-w-which way do we go now?' Diek asked, beginning to feel the weight of the box under his arm.

'We're ahead of them, so we have to keep moving down.'

'Right . . .'

'You see that big mountain, the one that sticks out?'

'Yes, it looks very . . . familiar.'

Burnie nodded.

'That's the Twelve,' he said. 'We need to cut across the base of it, and keep it on our left until we hit Rintintetly Forest.'

'Oh,' said Diek, despondently. It all sounded a long way from Little Irkesome, the village he called home. 'And where do we go from *there*?'

Burnie started to run again.

'River Washin,' he called back. 'We find a boat, then get in it and row the damn thing all the way to Spittle.'

'Will we be safe in Spittle?'

'Dunno: but we'll last a damn sight longer in Spittle than we will out here in the wilderness. C'mon!'

Diek put on an extra sprint.

'Do you think they'll catch us?' he asked.

'Not likely. There's only two of us, and I reckon we slipped by them. Besides, they'll be far more concerned with taking the towns and cities, don't you think?'

'I suppose so.'

'Get to the boat-yard,' said a voice.

Diek glanced down at the box. 'What was that?'

'You gotta get to the boat-yard. Then you can nick an 'alf decent boat.'

'Where can we find a boat-yard?' yelled Burnie, catching Groan's comment.

'There's one of 'em at the bottom o' that

Rintintanomy place. It's got a few of 'em an' some good 'uns what Gordo an' me tried to nick a few years back. There's a troll what guards it, bu' I reckon—'

'A troll?' Burnie snapped. 'What the hell are we going to do against a ruddy great monster like that?'

Groan seemed to think for a moment. 'I could 'it it.'

'You're in a box,' Diek reminded him.

'Oh yeah. Er . . . maybe you could 'ide from it, then steal a boat an' get 'way quick.'

'It's possible,' Burnie admitted. 'Are the boats on land or are they actually moored at the riverbank?'

'Some of 'em were in the water, I fink.'

'Right,' said Burnie. 'Well, thanks for that: we'll certainly give it a go.'

'Are you serious?' Diek asked, glancing at him.

'Yes, I'm serious: a chance is a chance!'

'Get down! Get down!' Diek yelled suddenly.

The two companions dived for the cover of a nearby bush as the dragon swept over the clearing, its giant wings beating the air.

'Do you think it saw us?' Diek whispered.

'Who knows?' snapped Burnie. 'I didn't even see the damn thing until it was almost upon us!'

'Maybe it's just doing a scout of the area to make sure none of the warband got away.'

'Do you think any of them did?'

Burnie managed to keep the croak out of his voice as he whispered: 'Doubtful.'

'I'm sorry, Burnie. At least they . . . died heroes.'

As the little troglodyte sniffed back the sorrow, Diek peered out from the bush.

'They're not following . . .' he muttered, scanning the mountain path and listening hard.

'Mmm . . . what?'

'The zombies; they're not following. They must have reached the mountaintop by now, yet I can't see them *or* hear them approaching.'

Several minutes passed, but the dragon did not return, and no sound was heard from the mountain.

Burnie rubbed his gloopy chin.

'We cut out east, so I reckon they went down the other side. That would mean they're headed west, for Crust . . . and Little Irkesome. I don't doubt they've set their eyes on Legrash, to be honest.'

'Little Irkesome?' Diek's eyes suddenly widened. He let go of the box, which lodged precariously in the thicket. 'B-but that's where my mum and dad live! I've got to get home: I've got to!' He scrambled out of the bush and started to run down the path, but Burnie caught up with him and clung frantically to his leg.

'Wait, boy! You can't go haring off – you'll get yourself killed!'

'B-but it's my family!'

'They might be lucky: the army might not touch Irkesome!' Burnie managed to slow Diek down. 'And if

169

they're *not* lucky, then there's pretty much nothing you can do about it . . .'

'B-but I should be there . . .'

'Why? To get trampled and killed in line with everyone else who opposes them? That's an *obsidian dragon*, lad; an *obsidian dragon*. You don't fight *obsidian dragons* – you see one coming, you run away. Simple as.'

'I must . . .' Diek's eyes filled with tears, and he slumped on to the ground. 'If I was still possessed, I could do something . . . now I'm just a worthless cow-hand again.'

Burnie hurried over to retrieve Groan's box from the bush. Then he sat down beside Diek and put his hand on the boy's shoulder.

'Listen, lad: you don't have to have special powers to be a great hero! Just having the heart to do what's right makes you special enough.'

'Yes, but what can I actually do? When I was possessed—'

'You were under the influence of some higher power, Diek . . . and judging by the things you *did* under that influence, I wouldn't be at all surprised if it was Vanquish himself who guided you. Trust me, boy, you don't *need* that kind of power . . .'

'But it gave me command of things!'

'Yeah, rats and children.'

'Not just rats and children! Cows, chickens, wolves,

you name it! Now I'm back to being an ordinary, useless boy.'

Diek had clenched his fists and his cheeks were flushed with anger.

'I can't believe I went through that limbo hell of darkness just to come out an empty—'

'Stop.' Burnie had moved away from Diek, a look of wary apprehension on his face. 'Don't say another word . . . and calm yourself down.'

Diek took several deep breaths. 'I'm sorry,' he managed. 'It's not your faul—'

'I stopped you,' Burnie interrupted, 'because when you got angry just then, your eyes were glowing like a couple of burning embers. Are you *sure* you didn't bring anything back with you?'

Effigy Spatula stood on the battlements of Spittle's Marsh Keep, his friends standing either side of him. All three of them had exactly the same thing on their minds.

'It's a bit weird though, isn't it?' Jimmy said, looking out at the hustle and bustle of a city totally oblivious to the danger approaching it. 'I mean, why meet him up here?'

'Maybe he's got a magic ship that sails through the air or something,' Obegarde hazarded. 'I know it sounds unlikely, but still . . .'

'Do you get any vibes from him?' Effigy asked, eyeing the vampire carefully. 'I mean, you lot . . .'

'Reading minds, you mean? Oh, don't think I haven't tried, but Moltenoak's certainly not one for cracking. I have a strong suspicion that reading *his* mind might inadvertently trigger my own death.'

'Maybe you're right about the airship,' Jimmy said, carefully studying the sky. 'Maybe it's more like a balloon . . .'

'Gentlemen.'

The three companions turned as the hooded man emerged from the trap door. 'Are you ready to go to Dullitch?'

'Yes,' said Effigy, carefully. 'Is your . . . ship nearby?'

Moltenoak smiled. 'I don't have a ship,' he said. 'Nevertheless, I am going to transport you to Dullitch – extremely fast. You all know what you're doing when you get there . . .'

'Staying out of your way,' Jimmy said, working from the instructions Effigy and Obegarde had passed on. 'And getting into the palace – oh, and finding the soul-caskets.'

'Very good. Now, they may only contain one soul each – so there will probably be a good deal of them. Be sure to look out for strange jars, unusual bottles, etc. – these might also have been used. Take no chances whatsoever; where in doubt, smash everything. Do you think you can manage that?'

All three nodded.

'Yes,' said Effigy. 'You can rely on us.'

'I don't doubt it; do you have swords?'

Obegarde nodded. 'Two each, in fact.'

'Very well, gentlemen.' Moltenoak straightened himself out, and smiled. 'Then we shall talk no longer. Now . . . allow me to show you my *other* outfit.'

# Seven

Earl Visceral and his daughter, Vanya, strode through the corridors of Spittle's famed Marsh Keep, a half sunken fortress that the majority of the city's troops called home. Steward Lambontroff, still supported on a large and extremely comfortable-looking cushion, was carried along beside them by the polite but inept Mr Theoff.

'I notice we got the short straw,' he groaned, trying to twitch enough to dissolve the itch in his left nostril. 'A few hundred men against an obsidian dragon is pitiful . . . laughable, in fact.'

'I know that,' Visceral agreed, though at the same time trying to smile reassuringly at his daughter. 'Even I was against committing our troops to war, but we have to take a stand — we can't just allow this evil to overthrow our land.'

'You're doing the right thing, Father,' Vanya said, quickly adding, 'And I think you are very brave to make such decisions.'

Visceral leaned down and hugged his daughter.

'I love you, sweetheart,' he whispered. 'Take care of the kingdom for me.'

Vanya tried not to look at him as he kissed her forehead. She turned to the cushion instead.

'You're very brave too, Steward Lambontroff,' she said, sniffing back the tears.

'Yeah, well, bravery is my middle name,' Lambontroff lied, winking at the girl. 'You know, before I was . . . er, decapitated, I used to be a road-warden. It's a very interesting line of work; you get to meet all sorts, doing a job like that. You know, there was this one time when these three gangsters—'

'I sent another ravensage to Baron Muttknuckles,' Visceral interrupted, quietly indicating that his daughter should leave them. 'And, astonishingly, I received a reply. The baron tells me that he and his men are sailing east along the Washin. I must admit I'm surprised . . .'

Loogie sniffed. 'Yeah, well, at least Blood'll get some extra help — not that he bloody needs it with that barbarian leading his cause.'

'Do you think they'll win?'

'No . . . but they certainly stand more of a chance than us . . .'

They walked along in silence for a time, watching the soldiers on the floor below preparing for battle – assembling weapons, sharpening swords and putting on armour.

'Who is he, do you think? That stranger with the hood?'

'Moltenoak?' Visceral shrugged. 'I really don't know. All I know is that he seemed to have second sight, and that I was absolutely terrified to argue with him.'

'You and me both,' Loogie muttered. 'Mind you, a six-year-old kid could dropkick *me* over the battlements. Doesn't give you much confidence, really – being a head. It was a different story when I had a body, of course. You know once I . . .'

Visceral closed his eyes, and prepared for yet another embroidered yarn.


'But it doesn't make any sense!' Diek said. 'I'm not hearing the voices! I can't still have magic in me: I can't!'

He and Burnie had circumnavigated the Twelve and were in sight of the southern edge of Rintintetly Forest.

'Maybe it's just an afterglow or something,' Burnie hazarded. 'I mean, you *were* in another dimension. It'd be pretty strange if you came back with *nothing* to show for it.'

'Hmm . . . maybe that's why the broomstick worked! Do you think I can still charm animals?'

Burnie shrugged. 'How did you do it before?'

'With a flute.' He turned to the little troglodyte. 'Do you carry a flute?'

'Surprisingly enough, no,' Burnie admitted. 'Flutes seldom make my list of essentials when going to war.'

'Oh.'

They walked along in silence for a time.

'Groan's been very quiet,' Diek said, eventually. 'Do you think he's asleep?'

'Dunno,' said Burnie. 'Can you be asleep when you're just a voice?'

The little troglodyte stopped suddenly, grasping Diek's arm. 'Look,' he whispered. 'The other army! We've caught them up!'

The two companions looked down at the edge of Rintintetly Forest, where a vast sea of zombies were slowly marching north, towards Phlegm. The obsidian dragon wheeled in the sky above them, Gape barking unintelligible orders from its back.

'Let's slow down a bit,' Burnie muttered. 'It's going to be difficult enough getting into that boat-yard *without* attracting the attention of a damn war-horde.'

Diek nodded. 'I agree.'

'Me too,' said the box. 'Jus' be ready ta move when the last one ain't there no more.'

'Oh, hello Groan,' Diek replied. 'I thought you'd gone into hibernation or something: you haven't spoken for ages.'

'I ain't 'ad nuffin' ta say.'

The two companions glanced at each other, then returned their attention to the marching army.

'Bloody hell,' Burnie said suddenly. 'Will you look at *that*!'

Diek spun around.

A grim line of black clouds had settled over Dullitch, darkening the city and the land immediately surrounding it. Every few seconds, a fork of lightning would arc from the sky . . . and a distant rumble would be heard.

'It's not like any storm I've ever seen,' said Diek.

'C'mon, I want to get as far away from that place as possible.' Burnie sounded anxious.

'What about the army?'

'We'll be *careful*. C'mon!'

Burnie hurried off down the mountainside, Diek trailing in his wake with the box still thrust firmly under one arm.

Prince Blood and Viceroy Funk galloped through the Mountains of Mavokhan. Having decided that coaches would draw too much attention, the two rulers had set out on horseback, each accompanied by four of their most trusted soldiers. Grid Thungus had made it clear that he didn't want company and rode at the back of the group.

'My army will meet us on the Coldstone Plains,' said Prince Blood, still slightly shaken by the look Moltenoak had given him. 'I have sent ravensage to Baron Muttknuckles and the leaders of Crust, Irkesome, Chudderford and Shinbone, asking them all to do the same.'

'My own troops will join us en route to the plains,' Viceroy Funk added. 'I have also taken it upon myself to send word to Pegrand Marshall, the Steward of Fogrise, in case he has any men he can spare. Personally, though, I doubt it. Fogrise is not the place it once was: I think Duke Modeset pretty much ran it into the ground.'

'I liked Modeset,' Blood muttered. 'I wonder how he would have handled the current crisis.'

'Badly,' said Funk. 'Like he handled everything else.'

The two lords glared at each other, and rode on.

# Eight

Burnie peered out from behind a boulder and, checking that the coast was clear, dashed frantically to a similar rock that lay further down the path.

After a few seconds, Diek followed the same procedure and joined him there.

'It's going to take us all day, moving like this,' he complained, eyeing Burnie as if the little troglodyte had a screw loose. 'Can't we just make a run for the woods?'

'That's what we *are* doing!'

'Yeah, at a snail's pace!'

'Do you want us to get caught?'

'By who?' Diek glanced around. 'There's nobody out here!'

'Shh! OK, go then! Go!'

Diek hurried over the rocky path and stumbled a little as he negotiated some of the lower foothills. He tripped several times, nearly losing the box on more than one occasion, but he eventually reached the trees without major incident.

Burnie waited another minute or two, then followed suit, moving a good deal slower and being decidedly more careful on the rockier ground.

At length he arrived, still puffing and panting, beside the boy.

'Right,' Diek said, addressing the box. 'We're in the woods. Where now?'

'Dunno,' Groan boomed. 'Where 'bouts are ya?'

'Who knows?' Diek exclaimed. 'We're in the trees, aren't we?'

'We're at the southern edge of Rintintetly,' Burnie told him. 'Just west of the River Washin.'

'Yeah, well you wanna go east, then. Don't go norf or souf or nuffin'. Jus' go east.'

Burnie glanced behind him at the looming might of the mountain.

'So you're saying we just go in a straight line from the base of the Twelve – is that right?'

'Yeah . . . s'right.'

'OK.'

Burnie nodded and they crept into the forest, which seemed immediately to grow dark around them.

'Anything dangerous in here?' Diek asked the box, his hands beginning to shake.

'There used to be a load o' zombies,' Groan mumbled. 'But I reckon me an' Gordo prob'ly killed most of 'em.'

'Good.'

'Yeah, it was.'

'We're bound to get lost in here though,' Diek complained. 'I mean, the chances of actually locating this boat-yard must be—'

'It ain't 'ard to find,' said Groan. 'All you 'ave to do is folla the sound o' runnin' water. That'll get ya to the Washin an' the yard.'

'Of course,' Diek whispered. 'I knew that.'

'I dunno . . . some folk'd think you two were fick in the 'ead.'

'Nice,' Burnie muttered, low. 'That's a *real* insult coming from *him*.'

'Go left 'ere,' said Groan.

Burnie gawped at the box.

'Eh? How do *you* know: you can't even see where we are!'

'I've bin countin' yer steps.'

Burnie and Diek turned left and trudged on for a time.

'There's a right comin' up,' Groan advised. 'You'll miss it 'fya don' watch out f'rit. 'S wedged between two o' them bendy trees.'

'I can see it!' Diek exclaimed.

'Don' take it.'

'What?'

'Don' take it: I was jus' lettin' ya know it was there.'

Burnie rolled his eyes. 'I bet we die in here,' he muttered.

The two companions crept further into the forest.

'It's like one of those places you read about in fairy tales,' Diek said. 'You know, with the princess in the tower who lets down her hair.'

'S'all rubbish,' said Groan. 'Ain't no such fing as a princess 'n' a tower. I know; I've bin lookin'.'

'Sorry to contradict you,' said Burnie, watching the trees very carefully, 'but it's actually true: a friend of mine who lives on the outskirts of Shadewell reckons it was *his* cousin that climbed the tower and rescued her.'

'Really?' Diek looked at the little troglodyte in amazement. 'Where was the tower?'

'Somewhere in the middle of Shinbone Forest.'

'And the girl really let down her hair?'

'Yes.'

'That's incredible! Did they live happily ever after?'

'Sadly, no: when he got to the top of the tower, she ate him.'

'What?' Diek stopped dead, his jaw dropping. 'Are you *serious*?'

'Yep. Turns out she was a reflecticor: an evil, shape-changing witch that uses its magically-enhanced beauty to lure young men into its nest in order to devour them.'

'That's the most horrible story I've ever heard,' Diek finished.

'How'd your frien' know?' said Groan.

'Mmm?'

'Your frien'; how'd 'e know 'is cousin got eaten?'

'Well, funny you should ask th—'

'Shhh!'

Diek grabbed Burnie and pulled him close to the trunk of a large oak tree.

'What is it?' whispered the little troglodyte. 'You nearly gave me a heart attack!'

Diek put a finger to his lips.

'There's something coming . . .'

They hunkered down behind the tree, and waited.


'I feel like a ruddy errand boy,' Baron Muttknuckles grumbled. The poorest lord in the whole of Illmoor had been on a round trip through Shinbone, Shadewell and Crust. He was currently heading for Little Irkesome.

'I hope to gods that Blood and Funk have had more luck than I have,' he spat. He glanced over his shoulder at the two hundred-odd men riding behind him. 'I've got more *cousins* than that,' he added.

The captain riding with him made a face, but tried to smile, despite the baron's continuing tendency to put down his men. 'Couldn't you have asked your cousins to join us, my lord?'

Muttknuckles released a hand from the reins of his horse, and used it to pick his nose.

'Ha! Some hope. There's more loyalty and compassion in an *earwig* than there is in my family.'

'Oh, I see.'

They rode on in silence for a time.

'Do you think we have a chance against such a terrible enemy?'

Muttknuckles belched.

'Yeah – a fat chance. With the weapons we've got, we'd be lucky to *distract* them.'

The captain looked back at the four or five men that had come from the baron's own town of Sneeze. They didn't appear to be armed with *anything*.

'Can your soldiers not afford basic swords, my lord?' he asked, his eyes wide with shock.

'Nope. Most of them squander their money on food.'

'Ah . . . I see. And what of yourself? Are you armed?'

Muttknuckles grinned.

'Of course I am: I've got a saucepan and two chair-legs.'

'Er . . .'

'Don't worry: the chair-legs have got nails in them.'

The captain smiled, but he stared at the baron thoughtfully for some time before speaking again.

'Aren't you . . . *afraid*?' he managed.

'Me? Nah . . . don't give a monkey's.'

'Really, my lord? But we're against zombies, dragons and a dark god!'

'So? If we die, we die,' Muttknuckles growled. 'Besides, we've got it easy . . . you should have seen my mother.'

The captain didn't speak again until they reached Little Irkesome.

# Nine

The troll was huge, even judged against the standards set by its own peculiar breed. It stood about ten feet tall, and must have weighed a ton. Surprisingly, the creature made very little noise as it trudged through the wood, a raft supported on its vast shoulders.

'*That* is a t-t-troll?' Diek stuttered.

'Yep.'

'But that's *insane* . . . we can't fight that thing!'

'We don't *have* to fight it,' Burnie whispered. 'We have to steal a boat from it.'

'They go down 'fyou 'it 'em right,' said Groan, conversationally. 'Mind you, there was this one—'

'Shhh!'

The two companions had arrived on the edge of the boat-yard which, sure enough, bordered the riverbank.

The yard basically consisted of a rickety shack – presumably the troll's home – and a collection of (mostly broken) boats and rafts. An old man was also present, carefully inspecting the boats as if he intended to buy one.

'Maybe we can use that to our advantage,' Burnie pointed out.

Diek nodded.

'Eh? What's 'appenin'?'

'We've reached the boat-yard,' the troglodyte explained. 'And there's a customer, there: an old man. The troll is heading over to talk to him.'

'I think we should try to get over to the river,' said Diek. 'That way we'll be concealed from the main yard by the bank! Besides, there's bound to be a few rowing boats moored on the river itself.'

'Good plan: I'll go first.'

Burnie moved through the grass, propelling himself with his elbows. Diek thought the little troglodyte looked like a snake as he proceeded towards the riverbank. Still, on the positive side, the troll didn't see him.

When Burnie was safely over the bank, it was Diek's turn to move.

'I'm going to have to use the trees,' he muttered to Groan. 'I can't crawl through the grass with your box under my arm – it'd take us twenty years to get there!'

'Yeah,' Groan agreed.

Diek took a deep breath and made to dash for the nearest tree, but just as he did so the troll turned round and headed straight towards him. Diek froze, still in a crouched position, wondering whether the monster had heard him. However, the troll promptly disappeared inside the shack, giving him a golden opportunity to run . . . and run fast.

Keeping a careful eye on the boat-yard's only customer, Diek Wustapha sprinted across the edge of the yard and literally dived for the riverbank, rolling out of control in the process. Fortunately, Burnie snatched hold of his arm before he plummeted into the unfriendly waters of the Washin.

'We did it! We actually di—'

'Shh!' Burnie grimaced at the boy. 'We can still get caught, you know!'

Diek nodded, and tried to calm himself as he peered round at the boats on offer. Most of them had been pulled on to the bank itself, presumably because they leaked or because pieces of them were missing. One rowing boat, however, was tethered to the bank by a thin rope. Not only did it look exceptionally seaworthy, it was also cluttered with all manner of strange-looking objects.

'Must belong to the customer,' Burnie whispered. 'What do you reckon?'

'I think we should steal it.'

'Me too. I'll get in, and—'

'No! You free the line, *I'll* get in.'

'Why?'

'Because I'm a damn sight smaller than you are, and I'll make less noise. *You* can jump in when I've got it on its way – very *quietly*. Now give me the box.'

Diek sighed, and did as he was told. Then he crept over to the boat and untied it while Burnie carefully stepped inside and grabbed hold of the oars.

The knot was tough, but Diek eventually managed to fathom it.

'Right!' he whispered. 'Go! Go! Go!'

The little troglodyte heaved on the oars. At the same time, and to Burnie's horror, Diek splashed loudly into the water and gave the boat an almighty shove, rolling inside at the last moment.

'What are you doing? Quietly, we said! Quietly!'

There was a commotion from the boat-yard, and the old man appeared on the riverbank. He was yelling at the top of his voice, and jumping up and down like a madman.

'Thieves! Thieves! They've taken my boat! Thieves!'

'We're borrowing it!' Burnie shouted back, as Diek replaced him at the oars. 'Honestly!'

The old man was soon joined by the troll, which promptly waded into the river and began to pursue them, its immense bulk fighting against the flow of the water as it waded on.

'Look at that!' the little troglodyte cried. 'It's actually

coming after us! We're dead meat – and all because *you* decided to make that kamikaze leap and splash through the water! Look what you've done! Look what you've done!'

Diek ignored him, and threw all his weight behind the oars, heaving them back and driving them forward with every last gasp of his strength.

Still, the troll was gaining, its stone legs cleaving through the water and its great arms reaching for the back of the boat.

'Catch those thieves!' the old man was screeching from the shore. 'Catch 'em! Catch 'em!'

Burnie was rummaging desperately through the clutter of bric-a-brac in the back of the boat. Not finding anything particularly offensive, he settled for a jolly-looking banjo.

'Oi!' shouted the old man. 'Put that down! That's mine.'

Burnie hefted the banjo in both hands, then climbed on to the edge of the boat and swung it out wide. It hit the troll's outstretched arms . . . and broke into splinters.

'My banjo! You scoundrels! You rotten despoilers!'

'Row faster, damn it!' Burnie screamed, but he could see that Diek was growing weary.

'I c-can't,' the boy managed. 'I'm getting tired.'

The troll made a sudden lunge for the boat, missing the prow by a gnat's wing, and tumbled face-first into the river.

Diek gave one last valiant pull on the oars, then slumped in the boat, exhausted.

'It's getting up again!' Burnie shouted. 'Look!'

'I . . . give up,' said Diek, weakly.

The troglodyte had continued his search through the boat's junk-pile, stopping at intervals to throw anything that looked even vaguely solid at the recovering troll.

'Wait!' Diek shouted, suddenly. 'Don't throw that one!'

Burnie hesitated, looking at the object clasped in his hand.

'Why? It's a stick with holes in it!'

'It's a *flute*. Give it to me . . .'

'What are you going to do, play it a tune?'

Diek lunged forward and snatched the flute from Burnie's hands. 'No,' he said, breathlessly. 'I'm going to see if glowing eyes are all I kept from my days as a charmer.'

The troll had risen from the depths of the river, and was once again striding purposefully towards the little boat. Roaring with anger, and spurred on by the furious screams of the old man, it brought its plate-sized fists down on the river, showering the thieves with water.

Diek put the flute to his lips . . . and began to produce a tune. It had been an age since he'd played, yet it felt so natural – and the music was *good*.

'Well, that's that question answered,' Burnie snapped at him, still looking for a weapon amongst the heap.

'Your charm-noise is doing absolutely nothing: the troll is still coming . . . and it looks more determined than ever.'

Diek closed his eyes and played on, praying to the gods that something, *anything* would heed the tune.

'Right,' Burnie muttered, plucking a makeshift drum from the bottom of the pile. 'This will have to do.' He raised the crude instrument above his head . . . and gasped.

Two crocodiles had appeared on the near bank. Slowly, languidly, they slipped into the water. They were headed straight for the boat.

'Er . . .' Burnie began, but when he looked back at Diek he saw that the boy had his eyes open, and was watching the scene with mounting glee.

Just before they reached the boat, both crocodiles suddenly changed direction, twisting through the waters en route for the troll.

Sensing the impending clash, Burnie dashed over to Diek and shoved him aside, taking hold of the oars in the process.

The first crocodile snapped at the troll, who drove a fist into the water beside it. Unfortunately for the troll, the crocodile took this opportunity to snap hold of his wrist. Before he could retaliate the second crocodile arrived, closing its jaws around his remaining arm. There followed a series of splashes as the troll heaved both beasts out of the water and began to flail around.

Fortunately, all this gave Burnie and Diek enough time to put some serious distance between themselves and the boat-yard.

Diek's music had saved them both.

'How did you *do* that?' Burnie cried, heaving on the oars with all his might. 'I mean . . . what did you actually DO?'

'The same thing I did when the voice was commanding me,' Diek said quietly. 'But . . . on my own.' He glanced up at Burnie, and smiled. 'I just searched the area for . . . a mind. It has to be simple, I think – not complex, like a human's. Then it's just a case of *feeling* myself take over. Somehow, that must all come out in the music . . . it's very odd.'

Burnie grinned.

'It's not odd,' he said. 'It's bloody amazing.'

# Ten

Two possessed sentries stood before Dullitch's great Market Gate, their hollow eyes fixed upon the River Washin. They didn't see the shape looming over them, or the fact that three figures detached from it, dropping on to the grasslands and rolling as they landed.

Jimmy, Obegarde and Effigy met up in the long grass, crouching just low enough to avoid detection.

'That was incredible!' Jimmy gasped. 'Can you believe that? I mean, can you actually *believe* it?'

'I believe it now,' said Obegarde, shaking his head. 'Great gods . . . and I always thought *I* was a special case.'

'It was . . . an experience I would never have thought possible,' Effigy agreed. 'But we still have a job to do – so

let's not upset our powerful new friend by doing it *distractedly.*'

'Agreed.'

'Yeah.'

Effigy peered over the top of the grass at the two zombies standing guard.

'They're about as observant as a pair of posts,' he muttered. 'We'll take *them* out first, then we'll head to the palace. Remember, all we're doing is looking for these containers: nothing else.'

Jimmy and Obegarde nodded, and the three of them crept through the grass towards the city.

Vanquish sat on the great throne of Dullitch, his head bowed in silent contemplation. The rest of the chamber was empty, though several possessed guards were manning the corridors.

A low hum accompanied the powerful ring of glowing colour that was forming in the air around the dark god's temporary form.

*Something is blocking me,* he thought. *I should be able to see all . . . yet I cannot. Dullitch is crystal clear . . . but the rest of Illmoor is a mist-shroud . . . What magic exists to challenge my own . . . What power still lies in this decayed land . . . ? None that I know of . . . so . . . why is . . .*

'Master . . .'

*A voice . . . out there, in the night.*

'Master . . .'

Vanquish started; the magic faded away, and his eyes flicked open.

A possessed servant was standing before him, almost bent double.

'**Yes?**'

'I have excellent news, master. The dragons are returning!'

'**Nonsense. I have not called upon them to do so.**'

The zombie produced a telescopic device and raised it before his master as evidence.

'I have seen them through this!' he said, his voice taking on a pleading edge. 'They return!'

Vanquish rose to his feet, an irritated yet quizzical expression playing on his face.

'I ordered them to lead the assault,' he muttered, snatching the telescope and slapping the zombie aside. He strode over to the palace balcony and climbed up the steps in order to get a clear view over Dullitch.

Putting the telescope to his eye, he scanned the skies.

The dragon was still no more than a shape on the horizon, but Vanquish didn't need a telescope to recognize that it was huge . . . his extraordinary sense told him as much.

'**That is not an obsidian dragon**.'

'It isn't, master?'

Vanquish stared up at the sky, his eyes blazing in sudden, ferocious anger. '**That**,' he said, slowly, '**is**

**Moltenoak . . . the first dragon I ever created. He is . . . an enemy.'**

The servant's eyes filled with tears. 'Will he destroy you, master?'

Vanquish smiled.

**'He will try.'**

# Part Three
# The Coldstone Conflict

# $\mathcal{O}ne$

Coldstone was aptly named – a flat barren plain where neither man nor beast rested easily. It was generally avoided by travellers, not because it housed any hostile creatures nor suffered from any particularly bad weather conditions, but simply because the whole place felt oppressive and despairing.

Yet it was on these plains that the soldiers of Illmoor joined to fight for their freedom.

Prince Blood, Viceroy Funk and their colleagues had managed to assemble an army of close to a thousand men. Even taking into account the large number of deserters, it was still a breathtaking sight. The troops ranged out across the plains in organized ranks, their

swords, axes and pikes glistening in the morning sunshine.

Grid Thungus rode up to the lords, drew his own great axe and pointed west.

'Who are they?' he asked, indicating an approaching warband of some two hundred riders.

Prince Blood squinted at the new army as they split from their two-man command group and joined the main body of troops on the plain.

'Baron Muttknuckles' men, I suspect. Ah, yes . . . here he comes now.'

Muttknuckles galloped up to the lords and gave a desultory nod of the head.

'Morning,' he managed. 'Nice one for a scrap, I reckon.'

Grid Thungus smiled as the rest of the lords muttered under their breath.

'Morning to you, Baron,' he growled. 'I don't suppose you remember me . . .'

Muttknuckles snorted at the big barbarian.

'Nope. Should I?'

'Possibly: I once robbed your keep . . .'

'Ha! That narrows it down – half the men in Sneeze have robbed my keep. Did I catch you?'

'No, but you did run after me yourself, on foot in fact! I was always impressed by that.'

'Yeah, well. Whatever. Who are ya?'

'This is Grid Thungus,' Prince Blood interjected.

'He will be leading our army into battle.'

'Yeah?' Muttknuckles raised an eyebrow. 'Says who?'

The barbarian shrugged, but his smile remained. 'Says me.'

The other two lords fell back a bit, talking quietly to each other.

'So,' Muttknuckles continued, squaring up to the new general. 'Any sign of the enemy yet?'

'No,' said Thungus. 'But I'm not surprised. The Gleaming Mountains are a nightmare to cross, especially if you're going *through* them rather than skirting the damn things.'

'Why *did* they go through them?'

'Because they already have another army heading north.'

'To Spittle?'

'Yes, but Earl Visceral's army is going to try to stop them at Phlegm.'

'Who's leading that lot?'

'Earl Visceral.'

'They're doomed, then – Visceral is a politician, he's not a warmonger.'

'He's going to try to hit them and run.'

'*Run?*' said Muttknuckles, sarcastically. 'Run where?'

'Here.'

'Oh . . . I see,' Muttknuckles rolled his eyes. 'So what you're saying is that halfway through one war, we're going to have a second one plough into us.'

Thungus nodded.

'Exactly; that's why we have to defeat the *first* lot quickly.'

Earl Visceral was riding south with a hundred men. Having left an equal number to form some (admittedly weak) resistance in Spittle, he was preparing to put Moltenoak's 'hit and run' plan into action. His nerves, which were frayed at the best of times, weren't being helped by the constant doubts being fired at him by Loogie Lambontroff, who had been thrust on the end of a war-pike and was being carried along by the clumsy Mr Theoff.

'I'm just glad they managed to find me a decent helmet,' he was saying. 'That way, if they find my skull on the battlefield, at least they'll think I was a normal, able-bodied soldier who got beheaded.'

Visceral took a deep breath and attempted to keep his patience. 'Can we at least try to look on the positive side?' he asked.

'I *was* looking on the bright side,' said Lambontroff, defensively. 'To be honest, I don't think they'll find me at *all*.'

'Get down! Now! We need to get to the bank!'

Burnie dropped the telescope he'd been using, then grabbed Diek and dragged him to the bottom of the boat. They'd enjoyed a largely uneventful trip up the

Washin thus far, but they had reached a point roughly halfway along its length where the river bent round and took them extremely close to Phlegm.

'What is it?' Diek managed, as Burnie stuck out an arm and began frantically to *lean* the boat into a change of direction.

'It's them! The black horde! The dragon! The walking possessed! It's all of them! I can't believe how slowly they're moving: we've actually caught them up!'

'What? Where?'

'Get DOWN, damn you!'

Diek pressed his face against the bottom of the boat.

'What are they doing?'

Burnie ignored the question, and employed one of the oars to steer the little boat towards the near bank. When the boat's prow kissed the muddy grass, he grabbed the telescope, nimbly hopped on to the bank and, crawling to the top, raised the device to his keenest eye.

'Oh great gods! There are thousands of them! They're about to attack Phlegm!'

'Let me see!' Diek clambered up the bank, remembering at the last moment to take Groan's box with him, and snatched the telescope from his companion.

Burnie waited while the boy moved it through several adjustments. 'Well? Can you see?'

Diek nodded. 'It's terrible,' he said, his voice

wavering. 'That dragon . . . the people of Phlegm don't stand a chance.'

'They must have gone through the forest, too,' Burnie added. 'Because they've got a tree as a battering ram – and I'm betting it will do the job.'

The horde of the possessed ground to a standstill a few metres from the great doors of Phlegm. For a few seconds there was stony silence. Then the enormous dragon crashed on to the dirt before them, and Gape Teethgrit dismounted. The great casket of souls was brought forward, causing the twenty or so zombies who had hold of it to stagger beneath the weight.

'People of Phlegm,' he thundered, in a voice filled with malice that rang out in the surrounding hills and valleys. Diek almost dropped his telescope. 'You are granted this one chance to surrender your souls and join the ranks of our lord, Vanquish. Otherwise, you shall die . . . crushed beneath the wrath of our might. I ask you now: will you surrender?'

The soldiers on the battlements of Phlegm maintained their stance. Nobody moved.

*They must be terrified,* Diek thought, watching the scene. *Absolutely terrified.*

Then a cry echoed from the top of the wall.

'We will not surrender. In the name of our absent king, and the royal steward who serves him, we shall fight you with the last gasps of our breath.'

Diek looked on in terror as Gape strode back to the

dragon and remounted it. The army behind him suddenly bristled with all manner of swords, axes, pitchforks, pikes and spears. Then . . .

'What's happening *now*?' Burnie asked.

'Wait!' Diek adjusted the telescope again, and slowly turned until he was almost facing the little troglodyte.

'What are you doing, lad? Don't play with the damn thing!'

'I'm not!' Diek muttered. 'There's some people over on the far hill, just right of the town. They're on horseback!'

'Really?' Burnie looked suddenly hopefully. 'Phlegmians, do you think?'

'I don't know. How do you tell?'

'Give it back to me, I'll tell you.'

Diek handed Burnie the telescope. The little troglodyte had barely put the device to his eye when he lowered it again.

'That's Earl Visceral, Lord of Spittle,' he said, excitedly. 'THAT'S the man I need to talk to.'

On a low hill just east of Phlegm, Earl Visceral turned to his commander in chief.

'Archers,' he said, looking on with grim determination as the order was passed on and more than seventy soldiers drew back their longbows.

'Ready when you are, Highness,' the commander said, nodding his head respectfully.

Visceral squinted at the army laid out before Phlegm. 'I want half the front line of zombies taken out,' he said. 'That should get their attention.' He leaned closer to the man. 'And be certain that you give the command to go the very *second* we get their attention. We will then have to gallop *in front of them* ... yes, I do mean *between them and the gates of Phlegm*, if we are to successfully draw them to Coldstone.'

The commander nodded, somewhat gravely, and urged his horse back along the line of archers. Raising a hand, he hesitated for a few seconds. Then he screamed: 'Fire!'

A rain of arrows flew from the seventy longbows, arcing through the sky with incredible speed.

For a second, Visceral and his men waited, with baited breath, their eyes fixed on the dark horde.

Then a wave seemed to wash over the sea of zombies as several of the creatures in almost every line on the front flank flew backwards, arrowheads embedded in their chests. The dragon turned its great head to scan for the new threat, as a roar went up from the soldiers who still stood on the battlements of Phlegm.

'With me now! With me!' screamed the commander of the Spittalian army, his horse thundering towards the space between Phlegm and its sprawling enemy.

Gape screamed out, and the dragon took to the skies. The army of the possessed charged forward.

\*   \*   \*

'Where are they going?' Burnie said, out of breath. He and Diek had reached the hill on which they'd expected to find Earl Visceral, only to find that he and his men had already charged away.

Diek put a hand to his forehead in order to block out the sun.

'It looks like they're galloping across the front of the horde.'

'But why would they do that?' Burnie cried. 'It's insane! They won't survive an attack from that rabble! They'll all be killed!'

Diek stood rooted to the spot as the inevitable clash loomed. The great dragon swooped, and the horde swept forward.

'Destroyed,' he said, his voice so low as to be almost inaudible. 'All those innocent people. It's not fair . . . I have to do *something*.'

Burnie watched the scene until it became clear that the dashing army were *not* going to make it through the gap. Then he closed his eyes and said a quiet prayer for the fallen. When he opened them again, Diek Wustapha had vanished, and the great dragon was twisting and turning in the air, as if caught in the throws of a fit.

# Two

A dirty black speck appeared in the air over the Plains of Coldstone. At first, it appeared to be moving on land. Then, as it drew nearer, it became clear that the dragon was aloft. There was no sign of the army beneath it, but every armed solider standing on the plains knew the horde was coming.

'Well, here goes nothing,' said Grid Thungus, taking up the reins of his horse and winking at the assembled lords. 'I bid you gentlemen good day, and I wish you the very best of luck.'

Muttknuckles glared at him. 'Deserting, are you?'

'Not at all,' said Thungus, pulling his great axe from its shoulder strap. 'I'm going to draw the dragon away from you.' He raised the axe above his head and began to urge the horse forward. 'If I were you, I'd have your men attack in one great rush. See? There really isn't anything to being a general . . . it's all about running at the enemy and hoping you don't get killed. Grant me luck, fellas! Hahaha!'

As the horse thundered away, picking up speed with every second, Muttknuckles turned to Prince Blood.

'I don't reckon much on his strategic skill,' he said. 'But I'll tell you one thing for certain: that bloke's got ba—'

'Yes,' Blood interrupted. 'But he's also just left *us* in charge of an army, so if you don't have any objections, I'm going to order a charge.'

'Not on all of them, you're not,' Muttknuckles warned. 'I'm taking a few hundred out wide so we can flank the scumbags.'

'Will that work?'

'It's something my grandfather taught me.'

Prince Blood hesitated.

'Your grandfather died in the opening salvos of the Third Crust Conflict,' he muttered.

'Yeah I know,' growled Muttknuckles. 'Somebody flanked him.'

'Diek? Diek! Where are you? Where did you go?'

Burnie, the box wedged under his arm, ran up and down the little hill, searching the landscape for Diek

Wustapha. His gaze took in the war-zone at Phlegm, the riverbank and even the series of small hills they'd run across in order to get to the earl. Then he saw the boy . . . and stopped dead.

Diek Wustapha was standing on the very top of the next hill, the flute at his lips. Burnie couldn't make out any sound because of the hideous din caused by the two clashing armies, but he knew instantly that Diek's actions were prompting the suddenly erratic flight pattern of the dragon.

Diek knew it, too . . . but he also knew that it wasn't working – not completely. The mind was far too strong . . .

'*How dare you try to break us,*' said a slithery voice in his head. '*We are older . . . so much olllder than you . . . we will not succumb to your low enchantments. We WILL NOT . . . WE WILL NOOOOOOT . . .*'

Diek felt a sudden surge of pain in his skull, and the flute fell from his hands. He staggered a few paces then folded up, dropping to his knees and crying out in pain.

'Diek!'

Burnie scrambled up the hill and hurried over to the boy, crouching beside him and throwing an arm over Diek's shoulders.

'You idiot! You can't mess with the mind of a dragon: they're the smartest breed of all!' He shook his head and fixed Diek with a stern glare. 'What did you think you were doing?'

Diek raised a shaking hand and pointed. 'That.'

The dragon's mental struggle had bought Visceral's men some much-needed time. As Burnie gawped at the conflict, a group of some fifty or sixty soldiers, Earl Visceral among them, broke free of the horde and galloped towards the River Chud.

The army of the possessed trampled the remaining troops, but were far too ponderous to give immediate pursuit. Still, Gape screamed at them . . . and slowly they reformed in order to follow the troop.

'It worked!' Burnie cried. 'I can't believe it: you actually helped them to get away! Well done, boy! Well done!'

But Diek's face had suddenly become a twisted mask of horror.

'The dragon!' he screamed. 'I've attracted its attention: it's coming this way!'

He staggered back.

'Run,' Burnie mouthed. '*Ruuuuuunnn!*'


Dragon-hunters had always been few and far between. This wasn't because the job paid poorly or because there wasn't much demand for such a talent: it was mainly because dragon-killers didn't live very long. A job which inevitably involves a good chance of your own death is a job not many people decide to make their own. In Illmoor, dragons were now a rare species. Occasionally, the odd cave dragon might make itself known but, by

and large, the breed was fast disappearing. Consequently, there were only two dragon-hunters at large in Illmoor, and of those two only one had ever actually taken on a dragon and beaten it.

His name was Grid Thungus. Born into a barbarian tribe not dissimilar to the Teethgrits' own brood, Grid had grown up with a grim certainty that life was short. He had therefore decided to set forth with a great axe and make it a lot shorter for things he didn't like. A curious attitude, but one that was remarkably common in his family.

Grid Thungus was a dragon-hunter. In his lifetime, he had fought three cave dragons, a slime dragon, two ice dragons and a Frecklin Wyvern. Admittedly, he hadn't beaten them all – but he *had* lived to tell the tale and that, in itself, was a testament to his talents.

The thing wheeling in the sky above him, however, was an obsidian dragon. It looked almost as old as Moltenoak . . . and that meant it was *olllld.*

Grid sighed despondently: it was clear that he had only one reasonable chance of getting out of this battle alive.

He thrust a hand into his loincloth, and produced a long, white handkerchief. Then he raised it high above his head . . . and waved it in the air.

A collective gasp went up from the Army of Illmoor ranged behind him: their appointed general was surrendering!

The dragon flapped noisily in the air. As Gordo struggled to bring the great beast to ground, the horde of the possessed began to appear in the distance, a vast line of the staggering soulless, stretching out as far as the eye could see.

Thungus forced his reluctant horse to approach the dragon.

'You surrender so readily,' said the voice of Gordo's inhabitant-spirit. The glowing eyes looked out at the Army of Illmoor. 'Who are *you*, to do so on behalf of so many?'

Grid Thungus smiled. 'I'm nobody special,' he said. 'But I *do* like your dragon.'

From his place at the head of the army, Prince Blood looked on in astonishment as the distant figure of Thungus slipped from his horse and bolted towards the dragon. Blood must have blinked then, for when he next looked upon the scene, Thungus was a darting blur and the dragon had taken to the air once again, its rider and the army's barbarian general struggling frantically in the saddle.

Grid Thungus had met Gordo Goldeaxe a fair few times. He tried not to let his fond memories of the dwarf affect the force with which he drove his head into Gordo's chin.

There was a crack, and Gordo's head snapped back.

Throwing a punch of his own that missed by a mile, the dwarf then tried to grab for his battleaxe, all the while keeping a tight hold of the dragon's rein with his free hand. His battleaxe slipped from its strap and dropped away. Grid almost lost his own, but managed to snatch hold of it at the last second.

Desperate to shake the attacker off, the dragon rose into the air and then spun itself around, causing Gordo to hang desperately from the reins and Thungus to hang desperately from Gordo. Still clinging on to his great axe with one hand, Thungus managed to clip the weapon on to his belt. Then, clamping a firm hold on the dwarf's stout legs, the barbarian began to climb, driving his knees into Gordo's back at every opportunity.

Meanwhile, far below this aerial battle, sensing that his troops expected something of him and realizing that the inevitable moment had arrived, Prince Blood forced his own horse over to the far edge of the army.

'Charge!' he shouted. 'Everyone! *Chaaaaargge!*'

There was a moment of hesitation, and then the Army of Illmoor cannoned towards the enemy. The speed of their assault almost took Blood's breath away, and he gasped with unexpected pride at the fury of his own soldiers. Slowly, very slowly, he began to urge his horse into a gallop.

Up in the skies, the dragon was still falling, spinning faster and faster as it hurtled towards the ground. At the last second it levelled out and furiously beat its wings, avoiding the stony plain by no more than a couple of metres before it took to the skies again.

Unfortunately for the dragon, the only thing it lost as a result of the dive was its rider. Gordo, who'd been hanging from the end of the reins, hit the ground hard, skidding along on the dirt for several metres before the friction stopped his progress. The dwarf quickly struggled to his feet, snatching a sword from a passing warrior and thrusting it into the man's chest with a defiant scream. He may have lost his mount . . . but he wasn't going to lose the battle.

Grid Thungus clung to the dragon's back like a leech, his great arms locked with every ounce of effort he could muster. Very slowly, he began to claw his way towards the saddle.

Air rushed around him.

The dragon, infuriated by the itch it couldn't scratch, dived once again, determined to take out its anger on the human army below it.

# Three

Moltenoak was the biggest dragon ever to exist in Illmoor; a crimson beast of such gargantuan size that he actually blocked the light of the sun for several seconds as he passed over the Crest Hill Tower. At once the most magnificent and most terrifying sight imaginable, Moltenoak came to ground inside the gates of the palace, transmuting into his human form in a fierce and blinding flash of energy.

First, there would be talk: Vanquish knew this with a certainty, for he had conceived and created Moltenoak himself: this creature and *all* its kind. They had been the perfect warriors during the continent's first war with Bobova, the founding father of light. They had also been the greatest companions, the most blessed of sons . . . until this wretch – this firstborn child – had betrayed him.

Vanquish stared down from the balcony at the approaching figure.

**You come here to beg forgiveness** . . .

The hooded man threw off his cowl and stared back.

*I come here to offer you death.*

**You** . . . **whom I gifted birth** . . .

*And a will of my own.*

. . . **in whom I bestowed magical blood** . . .

*Independent of yours.*

. . . **an ability to conceal your true form** . . .

*And a skill in shielding the land from your cruel eyes.*

**You betrayed me** . . . **in my hour of need. You sided with the light** . . . **and tricked me into a prison that has held for time uncounted! I curse you, Moltenoak! I** *made* **you** . . . **and you betrayed me!**

*You would have covered the land in darkness.*

**I still will** . . .

*Not while I draw breath.*

**Then** . . . **you shall draw it no longer.**

Vanquish extended his hand . . . and a burning spear of red light shot from his fingers.

Moltenoak raised his own hand and absorbed the ray, flinching only slightly as he took the force of it.

*Really, master. You insult me with such weak magic.*

Vanquish sneered.

**A taster, my child. That and nothing more.**

The dark god turned and ran, shoving two of his possessed servants aside as he went.

Moltenoak resumed his true form, and flew into the palace with such force that a gaping hole was left in his wake.

Landing on the flagstones of the devastated throne room, he released a jet of flame that melted the stones of the far wall as easily as if they were made of candle-wax.

But Vanquish was nowhere to be seen in the corridor beyond.

Burnie and Diek ran.

To say that they ran fast would have been an incredible understatement: Burnie and Diek ran for their lives. Perhaps crucially, they ran in opposite directions.

Diek dashed across the hills towards the River Chud, unintentionally following Earl Visceral's army, while Burnie reached the west bank of the Washin, and bolted south. However, he soon skidded to a halt when he realized, to his horror, that the beast hadn't pursued him.

*Not the boy*, he thought. *Not the boy!*

Burnie watched the great beast . . . and tried to follow it.

The dragon wheeled in the sky as it made to pursue Diek, its mind still burning with anger.

*Charm us, would you? Insignificant, mortal wretch. Now
you will be consumed . . .*

Diek ran on, his own thoughts racing. He
remembered being bullied by a few of the village boys
when he was growing up back in Little Irkesome, and
being pelted with stones on his way home from the
market. He also remembered the advice his dad had
given him: never to run in a straight line.

Diek didn't look behind him: he knew that to do so
would mean instant death. Instead, he began to run in a
series of zigzags towards the out-hanging edge of
Rintintetly Forest.

Just as he reached the trees, several of them exploded
in great gouts of flame. Diek dived for cover, scrambling
further into the forest as the shadow of the beast fell
across the hill beyond.

He gasped with relief. He'd made it – the dragon
couldn't follow him inside.

*Wrong.*

The dragon charged into the trees, its incredible bulk
forcing several of them over.

Diek turned and ran as the dragon charged again,
and again, and again.

*I will find you, human. It doesn't matter how long. it takes.
I will find you, if only to watch you burn . . .*

The voice was full of malice . . . and Diek couldn't
shake it from his head. He ran deeper into the
forest, but he could still hear the beast crashing through

the undergrowth behind him.

*Ah . . . so you delay me . . . clever . . . very clever – but pointless. My army shall catch up with the riders – wherever they go – and they shall destroy them . . . as I shall destroy you.*

The dragon had slowed to a careful crawl. It moved between the trees, its great wings folded up behind it. Every few seconds its scaly head turned to study the view in each direction.

Diek was crouched inside a tree hollow, shaking like a leaf, as he felt the beast moving closer. He nearly jumped out of his skin when a warty palm closed over his leg.

'*Aghghh!* Oh, Burnie, it's you! You scared me half to death!'

'Shhhh! I can see it . . . it's just over there.' The little troglodyte crept over to crouch in the hollow with Diek. 'That was a very brave thing you did, back there,' he managed. 'Stupid, but very, very brave.'

'I can't believe you came back for me!'

'Hey, of course I did. We've been through some tough stuff together, haven't we?'

Diek sighed, a world-weary look on his face.

'What now?' he breathed. 'If we try to move, that *thing* will annihilate us . . .'

'I think we should stay where we are,' said Burnie. 'At least for the time being. It's bound to give up the search . . . eventually.'

'But it can get inside your head,' Diek whispered. 'Maybe it knows where I am and it's just toying with me.'

'If someone don' tell me what the 'ell's goin' on,' said a voice, 'I'm gonna be kickin' some serious face when I get out of 'ere.'

'Shhhh!' Burnie and Diek exclaimed, looking down at the box in the troglodyte's arms. 'Keep it down! There's a dragon hunting us.'

'Fort so.'

Diek and the troglodyte shared a glance, then they hunkered down in the tree hollow and prepared for a long wait.

Visceral's cavalry thundered through the hills as if they were being granted speed by the gods themselves.

'We make for Chud Bridge,' screamed the earl, his eardrums pounding as loudly as the hooves thundering beneath him. 'Once we're over the river, it's Coldstone – and every man for himself. We fight for Spittle!'

'For Spittle!' shouted the captain beside him.

The cry was echoed by the rest of the cavalry, as the river and the bridge loomed into view.

# Four

The battle was raging into an inferno as the Army of Illmoor collided with their possessed countrymen. Swords clashed, axe-heads cleaved bone and pikes speared flesh as each side held back absolutely nothing in their determination to claim victory over the other.

Large numbers of warriors from either side staggered around blindly, wreathed in flame.

Far above them, the dragon was becoming increasingly frustrated with its human parasite. Try as it might, it couldn't actually shake the infuriating creature.

Grid Thungus had decided that he'd wasted enough time merely irritating his host. Keeping one hand firmly looped through the dragon's saddle-harness, he reached down and plunged the other into his boot, withdrawing a long dagger from the fur-lined recess. Then, waiting for the beast to draw level once more, he swung himself up into the saddle, raised the blade with both hands and brought it down into the dragon's neck.

The creature gave an almighty roar, and fell from the sky like a stone down a well. Grid Thungus hooked the reins around his neck . . . and prepared for a crash-landing.

Several screams erupted from the battle below as some of the more perceptive soldiers realized that the dragon was heading for the ground, fast. Within seconds, a large vacuum had opened in the midst of the conflict.

It was filled with a sound like the collision of two mountains. The entire land shook as the dragon landed.

Grid Thungus, who had leaped from the beast mere seconds before it came to ground, struggled to his feet and drew his great axe from its shoulder strap.

'Right,' he muttered to himself. 'Now for the difficult part.'

The battle was beginning to go against the Army of Illmoor. Possessed warriors were cutting down soldiers left and right, and those who did manage to gain the upper hand were finding their opponents increasingly difficult to put down. A second wind was badly needed.

It came in the form of Baron Muttknuckles. Leading a group of some two hundred cavalrymen, he ploughed into the right flank of the possessed army, his troops lashing out with everything they had. None fought more furiously than the baron himself, who swung out with a frying pan and practically decapitated the first zombie with the affront to attack him.

'Get out of it, you privileged scum!' he cried, clunking random troops with the chair-leg he carried in his other hand. 'Take my town, would ya? Take the shirt off my back as well, I'll bet! Have at ya!'

Grid Thungus circled the dragon wearily, looking for an opening. He found one, but just as he was about to strike the beast uncoiled, lashing out at him with claws and teeth.

Thungus moved with remarkable speed for his size, leaping left and right in order to avoid the attack. When the first jet of flame erupted from the dragon's nostrils, he had already rolled beneath it and was about to swing his great axe into the beast's stomach.

Another deafening roar resounded across the plain as the axe-head slashed its terrible wound across the scaly underbelly.

Recognizing the possibility of a collapse, Thungus somersaulted between the dragon's back legs, slashing the tendons on one of the giant appendages as he rolled out.

The dragon's last roar was the loudest of all. As the almighty beast collapsed in the dirt, Grid Thungus scrambled up its back like a spider and brought his axe round in an outlandishly wild sweep.

An incredible silence settled over the battlefield, and both armies took a step back from each other as the dragon's head rolled away from its body.

Soldiers and zombies alike lowered their weapons in shock.

Then Earl Visceral arrived.

Regaining his human form, Moltenoak strode through the twisting corridors of the wreckage that Dullitch Palace had become. Still, there was no sign of Vanquish.

**You won't find me.**

*I don't need to find you . . . I only need to keep you from escaping.*

**Fool! I could extinguish you with a blink of my eye.**

*Yes. Curious then, that you choose not to. Unless . . . unless you cannot extinguish me because that eye is not yours to blink.*

**You wish it were so.**

*I know it is so. We both know that you are not complete . . . and that the one thing you have hungered for is a return to your own body. Ha! What use is a soul when its true host is still hidden from it? Had I not been alerted to your return by the humans, you may have yet discovered the location . . . but your lack of subtlety sold you short.*

**I . . . can still uncover the location.**

*Unlikely. That is why the trick was perfect . . . that is why there were always two prisons for you, Vanquish. You may have found a way out of one, but you will not be able to locate and free the other. You have lost, my old master. You have lost.*

Moltenoak rounded another bend in the corridor, a smile playing on his lips.

*Look out now, Vanquish, look out upon Illmoor. I will give you one small glimpse of the land without attempting to block your mind. There . . . can you not see the battle at Coldstone? My own suggestion, that was. One dragon has already fallen . . . the other will soon join it. Tell me, master, do you still have enough power to sustain an entire army without the dragons to aid you? Ha! It will certainly be interesting to find out . . .*

A dark shadow fell across the doorway at the end of the hall, and Vanquish appeared.

'**So**,' said the dark god, his voice saturated with cruelty and malice. '**My body is at Coldstone, is it? You fool, Moltenoak. You always did talk too much** . . .'

Moltenoak transformed in the blink of an eye, his enormous frame splitting walls and bursting glass.

Vanquish threw up both hands and muttered under his breath, beaming with glee as an immense wall of ice developed in the air between them.

Thundering through the remains of the corridors, Moltenoak delivered a jet of white flame. It hit the wall and melted away more than half of it. A second burst removed the remaining ice, but Moltenoak was too late.

The body of Groan Teethgrit lay in a sprawling heap on the corridor floor. Vanquish had left his human host.

The great dragon bellowed with rage: he had made a terrible mistake.

# Five

Burnie looked down at the box in his hands: it was beginning to shake.

'Look,' he whispered, bringing it close to his lips. 'We're trying to hide from a dragon here – and if it finds us, it will kill us. So do you think you could keep still?'

'Eh?' said Groan's voice. 'What you talkin' 'bout? I ain't movin'!'

'Shh!' Diek urged, as he heard the beast crunching through the trees towards them. 'He's going to get us— Burnie, what's wrong?'

The troglodyte was holding on to the box with all his might, but it was still shaking violently.

'H-h-help me hold on to this!' he managed. 'It feels like it's going to explode!'

*Ah* . . . the dragon thought. There *you are.*

'It's found us!' Diek screamed out. 'Run! Run for the edge of the forest!'

He grabbed hold of Burnie and together they bolted towards the sunlight that played on the fringe of the trees. Diek practically had to carry the little troglodyte, who was clutching the box so hard that his entire body was trembling.

The dragon crashed along behind them, picking up speed with each giant stride. It felt the fires brewing in its stomach.

'Wha's 'appenin'?' Groan boomed, but the companions were too preoccupied to give an answer.

Diek broke from the wood, but got only a few paces before he felt a sudden resistance that caused him to stop. At first he thought the dragon was somehow blocking his movement. Then he turned around.

The box had begun to rise into the air, Burnie still clinging to it for dear life.

'Let it go!' Diek cried. 'Let the box go! The dragon's probably controlling it or something!'

''Ere,' said Groan. 'You talkin' 'bout me? Don' let me go! If you do, I could end up 'nywhere! 'Old on to me box!'

Diek grabbed hold of Burnie's leg, just as the hulking beast emerged from the woods.

The dragon charged up the hill and released a jet of flame that burned away the grass patch where Diek and Burnie had been standing. But the two companions had gone: they were now visible only as a small, airborne speck that rocketed into the distance.

*A tricky one you are . . . tricky, to be sure. But we love a challenge – we . . . thrive . . . on it.*

The dragon took to the skies, and thundered after them.

Earl Visceral's arrival on the battlefield had preceded the arrival of the second horde of the possessed. Now the Army of Illmoor was outnumbered, though they still fought valiantly to turn the tide against their mindless foes.

Grid Thungus swept across the battlefield, his great axe carving strange and terrible patterns as it cleaved everything in its path. Suddenly, he was alone in a widening circle of the possessed. Wondering why the enemy were suddenly giving him such a wide berth, Thungus turned on his heel and peered around.

Gape Teethgrit walked out of the battle and hesitated for barely a second before driving his longsword at the barbarian's throat. Thungus managed to block the thrust, but was driven back by the sheer strength of the brute.

*There's no doubt about it,* he thought. *You're Groan's brother all right.*

On the other side of the battlefield, Baron Muttknuckles was still beating everything that crossed his path with the nail-smothered chair-leg. Prince Blood had managed to avoid the conflict entirely and was watching from a nearby hill, attempting to assuage his own guilt by stopping several of his soldiers and ordering them away from the battlefield. Earl Visceral, on the other hand, was engaged in a bitter battle with two of the possessed. He fought for his friend, Viceroy Funk, who had fallen to the pair, a pitchfork buried deep in his back. He had been a good man . . . and a good leader. He deserved revenge.

Effigy, Obegarde and Jimmy Quickstint were enjoying a well-earned break from their determined effort to enter the palace. Having forced back every unit of the possessed they encountered (mostly due to Obegarde's incredible fighting abilities), they'd stopped at what remained of the palace gates in order to regroup and take stock of their situation.

As Jimmy made to lean against the once-grand arch, an explosion of sound caused the three companions to start.

Moltenoak erupted from the palace, his great wings beating furiously as he took to the sky. The giant red dragon sped through the air like a rogue cannonball, leaving a trail of curling smoke in his wake.

'What the hell?' Effigy gasped, hurrying off after the

dragon before he realized that doing so was futile. 'Where is he going? What's happening?'

Obegarde drew his sword warily, looking back towards the palace.

'Do you think he's done it?' he said. 'Do you think he's destroyed Vanquish?'

'What if he hasn't?' said Jimmy, doubtfully. 'He wouldn't just leave, would he?'

Effigy shook his head. 'I certainly hope not.'

The vampire let out a deep sigh. 'So what do *we* do?'

'Keep on with the plan, I suppose,' said Effigy. 'We need to get inside the palace and search for these caskets.'

'Yeah,' Jimmy agreed. 'After all, that's what he *told* us to do.'

'Look's like the decision's been made for us,' Obegarde finished, as a group of twenty possessed guards appeared in Oval Square. 'I know I only get one vote, but I'm voting we don't fight that lot . . .'

# Six

Moltenoak moved through the sky at lightning speed, his great wings working frantically as Illmoor slipped by far below him.

Soon, the battlefield would be in sight. Not soon enough, though – the mistake had been made. He knew he wouldn't, couldn't be in time to stop the unthinkable from happening . . .

Gape Teethgrit and Grid Thungus had fought each other to a standstill. Steel glinted off steel as the two warriors circled. Grid could tell that his opponent's mind possessed none of the barbarian's inherent skill, but it seemed to have full access to the vast reserves of

strength that were the Teethgrit family's stock in trade. He knew he had to go for a killing blow – but first he needed to get past the soulless fool's defences.

Grid charged forward . . . and stopped. The ground beneath him was beginning to shake.

Gape also swung out with his sword, but the quake caused him to topple.

Baron Muttknuckles and Earl Visceral likewise ceased their individual combats, as all across the battlefield warriors were looking down at the cracks appearing in the dusty plain.

From his position atop the hill, Prince Blood looked down on a scene of absolute chaos: the very ground was splitting beneath the battle, great chunks of it falling away as the land swallowed zombie and human alike.

Suddenly, one entire section of the plain fell in, taking with it more than a quarter of the army on both sides.

'Did you see that?' Prince Blood gasped, watching the events with mounting horror.

The officer on horseback beside him was speechless, his eyes locked on the disastrous collapse. Then his jaw dropped, and he pointed.

'Look, Majesty! LOOOK!'

Prince Blood followed his gaze, and gulped.

Something of unimaginable size was beginning to emerge from the hole.

# Seven

A large block of stone was shifted aside, and Jimmy
Quickstint rolled into the corridor beyond.

'It's always worth taking a short cut,' he said, winking at
Effigy as he and Obegarde followed him into the palace.

'I don't know why,' the vampire complained. 'We
could have stepped through the hole caused by Effigy's
explosion.'

'Yeah,' Jimmy admitted. 'Or the one caused by our
friend, the hooded man, who's really an age-old dragon
in disguise.'

'Will you two shut up and help me out, here?' Effigy
snapped, producing a roll of parchment from his jerkin
and quickly unfurling it.

'What's that?' Obegarde prompted, as he and Jimmy shuffled around to see over the freedom fighter's shoulder.

'It's a map of the palace.'

'Where did you get it?'

'Visceral gave it to me. Now, let's see, we're *here*, so the throne room is *that* way . . .'

'Do we want to go to the throne room?' Jimmy wondered aloud. 'I mean, what if Vanquish is in there?'

'Well, we just have to hope he isn't,' said Obegarde.

At the end of the corridor, Effigy indicated the left-hand path.

'We go up the stairs at the end, turn left, right, left and then we're practically on top of it. Easy or what?'

'Oh yeah,' Jimmy grumbled. 'Everything we do *looks* easy . . .'

The other two ignored him, and together they continued along the corridor.

As the shadow rose out of the ground, every head on the battlefield turned to face it. A giant black-bodied sphere; at first it looked more like a small planet than the ageless demon it truly was.

Someone screamed, an ear-piercing cry of terror that washed over the sudden silence of the battlefield.

Then, all at once, a series of tentacles lashed out from the sphere, fixing on the ground and moving the bulky mass over the plain at a remarkable speed. At the same time, a line formed across the length of the huge body and split open, revealing a single, vast yellow eye. The pupil was covered in mucus, but not enough for the cruelty within it to be disguised.

Panic spread over the plain like a disease as every man with enough sense to comprehend the threat turned and ran for all they were worth.

Soldiers who'd sworn never to relinquish their swords dropped them without a second's thought, praying they could reach safety before the hideous entity thought to consider them.

Some died in the crush, trampled by their own friends and brothers. Some stood frozen to the spot, too terrified to move.

And then it happened.

Vanquish looked down upon the people of Illmoor . . . and began to kill them, indiscriminately.

# Eight

Burnie felt as though he'd been fired from a cannon. Curled up like a foetus, his body wrapped entirely around the box, he flew through the sky at a rate of knots, Diek still clinging desperately to his leg.

'You should have let it go!' the boy screamed, his voice distorted by the rushing wind. 'Why d-didn't you just let g-go?'

Burnie was too shocked to say anything; he was also scared out of his wits.

Behind them, the dragon soared aloft, wondering why it couldn't catch them – despite the fact that it was moving at its top speed.

Far in the distance, the spires of Illmoor's capital city reached for the heavens.

'Dullitch!' Diek screamed. 'The box is taking us towards Dullitch!'

Burnie forced open one eye, only to have it immediately fill with water as it was battered by the wind.

'Is the dragon still behind us?'

Diek shivered and closed his own eyes, trying to keep his head from exploding.

'I th-think so. I can hear something flapping!'

Hills, mountains and rivers rushed along beneath them. Then they were hurtling over the city walls.

'The palace!' Diek cried. 'H-here comes the palace! Arghgghhhhhhhhhhhh!'

'What's that noise?' Effigy said, stepping through the wreckage of fallen masonry that lay strewn across the floor of the throne room.

'Eh?' said Jimmy, distractedly. He was searching an antechamber for likely-looking soul-vessels.

'There *is* a noise,' Obegarde agreed. 'I can hear it too. I think it's coming from . . . arghh! Effigy! Look out!'

The freedom fighter spun around, just as Burnie and Diek came flying through the dragon-made hole like a pair of rogue torpedoes.

There was a noisy collision, accompanied by several cries of pain, and all three ended up in a tangled heap

on the floor. The box hit the wall and exploded, a strange mist drifting from within.

'Effigy!' Obegarde shouted. 'Effigy, are you OK?'

Jimmy and the vampire rushed over to help their friend, but both quickly recoiled in shock.

'B-Burnie?' Obegarde said, his eyes lighting up. 'Burnie! It *is* you! Effigy . . . look who it is!'

Effigy Spatula forced himself on to his elbows, blood dripping from a wound on his temple. 'Hello Burnie,' he said . . . and fainted.

Jimmy was pointing at the boy, his eyes wide with shock.

'You,' he said, accusingly. 'You're Diek Wustapha!'

'He is,' Burnie said, struggling to his feet. 'But I want you to leave him be.'

'But he kidnapped—'

'Please, Jimmy . . . it's complicated. Right now, the only thing you need to worry about is—'

*Me?*

Everyone in the room heard the word, though it was unspoken, like a searing brand burned in their minds.

The dragon crashed on to the flagstones of the throne room, its great wings folding up behind it.

*You can't run any more, young enchanter. Now you and your pathetic friends will feel my wrath . . .*

'Run!' Diek spluttered. '*Ruuun!*'

Obegarde ran at the dragon, which clawed him aside

as if he were a child's toy: the vampire rocketed into the far wall and lay still.

Wasting no time, Jimmy was first to his feet. He'd almost reached the corridor when he realized the others weren't with him. Burnie and Diek were still in the centre of the room, attempting to carry Effigy's unconscious form between them.

'There's no time!' Jimmy screamed. 'It'll melt us where we stand!'

'Oh yeah?' said a voice behind him. ''Ow's it gonna do that if I've ripped its stinkin' 'ead off?'

# Nine

Vanquish moved over the plains, spidery legs carrying the immense bulk with comparative ease. Dark clouds gathered around him, appearing to fuel the chaotic god with lightning.

Vanquish dealt death in terrible quantities, his great eye firing a beam of jet-black liquid that instantly killed every living thing it touched. The corpses were then eaten by the beast, which dropped down upon them, lowered by the spider legs, and used an otherwise invisible set of mouths to consume them *whole*. All across the battlefield soldiers fled, were hit by the black spew and fell. Even the army of the possessed were destroyed in astonishing numbers.

'Retreat!' Prince Blood screamed, as Visceral and several other riders galloped past him. 'The battle is lost! Run for your lives! *Retreeeeeeeeat!*'

As the surviving troops swept away from the dark god, Grid and Gape staggered and fell. Caught together, they had both been completely covered in the black liquid. Life drained from the two great heroes, and Vanquish ate everything that was left behind.

It was then that Moltenoak arrived. Swooping down from the skies over Coldstone, the great dragon surrounded its former master in a burning ring of fire.

The dark god let out an unearthly scream and staggered slightly, before his legs managed to stabilize the bulk of his body. Vanquish shuddered terribly, and his yellow eye flicked upwards. Then he launched a fierce stream of death at the great dragon.

Moltenoak dived to avoid the blast, twisting through a wild arc as the liquid spew shot wide of its mark.

A spark of anger lit the dragon's gleaming eyes and it sent forth a jet of flame that seared a horrific wound across the dark god's central mass.

Vanquish took seconds to absorb the fire, before disgorging three separate sprays of its own dark death-ray.

Moltenoak swooped and swerved, only avoiding the final jet by the narrowest of margins. Then it dropped from the sky . . . and crashed into its maker with the fury of ages.

\* \* \*

Groan Teethgrit appeared in the throne room's devastated doorway.

'I 'ate dragons,' he said to Jimmy, as Burnie and Diek carried Effigy to the far end of the room. 'It don' matter 'ow many I kill, there's always anuvver one comes along, finkin' it's 'ard. Any o' you lot got a sword?'

Jimmy raised a shaking hand and placed his blade in Groan's giant palm.

'Looks all righ',' said the barbarian, calmly. 'Is it 'ny good?'

'Groan!' Jimmy screamed. 'The dragon! Can't you see it?'

'That thing? Yeah, but I seen 'em all before. They're rubbish. You lot bedda get out of 'ere, though.'

The dragon was snorting out plumes of smoke, feeling a deadly flame begin to brew in its stomach. It looked on, eerily passive as the group of humans hurried from the room, leaving their large companion behind.

The dragon's slit-like eyes widened: to its mounting astonishment, the warrior was walking *towards* it.

Feeling the flames rise up, the dragon rushed forward, breathing out a blanket of fire that engulfed both the room *and* the corridor beyond.

When the smoke cleared, the beast smiled with satisfaction at its victory: where the barbarian had been there was nothing but dust and ash.

The dragon's great eyes swept over the room, then

flickered and froze, a thin trickle of blood appearing at the corner of each pupil.

A sword was protruding from the top of its head. Plunged in beneath the jaw, the blade had eviscerated the dragon's brain.

Groan rolled out from beneath it, as Burnie and the rest of the group appeared at the entrance to the throne room's antechamber.

'S' like I said,' the barbarian boomed. 'I 'ate dragons.'

Burnie and Diek hurried over to Obegarde. To their relief, he was merely unconscious.

'It's OK,' Burnie called to Effigy, who still lay dazed in the doorway. 'He's breathing: he's going to be fine.'

'Effigy! Effigy!' Jimmy appeared from the depths of the antechamber, a look of delight on his face. 'I think I've found them: I think I've found the soul-caskets!'

Effigy Spatula dragged himself to his feet.

'C'mon, gang,' Jimmy continued. 'You too, Groany . . . I think we might need your strength to smash these open.'

# Ten

The battlefield was practically deserted, save for a few stragglers who'd either lost their horses or had deliberately decided to run away on foot.

Gordo Goldeaxe was among them – *he* woke up running.

'Wh-what? Where am I?' he shouted, skidding to a halt as he managed to reclaim his limbs. He glanced back at the battlefield, where a giant monster with swarming tentacles was locked in close combat with the biggest dragon he'd ever seen. Gordo blinked a couple of times, then shook his head to check that he wasn't dreaming. On the contrary, when he reopened his eyes the scene became much more vivid.

The two leviathans ripped great and bloody chunks from each other, Moltenoak's iron jaw working as ferociously as the razor mouths that had opened up all over the mass of Vanquish in order to consume his opponent.

The sound of the battle was like the rending of ten worlds, but it was certainly giving the battlefield's walking wounded a chance to stagger away from the scene.

Gordo's eyes watched the scene with increasing disbelief, but his mind had wandered as his memory had begun to return to him. There was a hammer . . . yes, a hammer . . . and . . . and Groan had been acting strangely. Yes, that was it! His best friend had attacked him!

'Groan? Where are you?' Gordo ripped his gaze away from the unreal horror before him and looked up and down the battlefield. The big barbarian was nowhere to be seen. Moroever, the entire plain was covered in some sort of dark discharge from the . . . *thing* on the ground. Gordo's mind swam with different terrors, some imagined and some real. Then he summoned enough sense to return his main attention on the horror at hand.

CRASH.

Gordo started as the dragon pulled its unspeakable enemy fell to the ground. From what he could make out, it appeared that the dragon had managed to clamber

atop the monster, causing the legs of the black mass to buckle beneath it.

Gordo shook his head in amazement, rubbed his prickly beard . . . and reached for his battleaxe. It was gone. *So much for fighting, then,* he thought. *Still, probably just as well. I don't fancy my chances against either of those things. If only Groan was here . . .*

Thanks to some much-needed help from Burnie and Diek, Jimmy had managed to smash every single jar, flask and bottle in the room. A lot of the vessels looked ancient; they just had to hope that they were the *right* ones.

'Hey,' Jimmy said, suddenly. 'Where's Groan?'

'I'm not sure,' Diek managed. 'I thought you asked him to help us?'

'I did! Where's he got to?'

Jimmy hurried back into the throne room, the others trailing behind him.

Groan was crouching beside the far wall. The wall itself, the only one bordering the throne room to remain completely intact, was glowing ever so faintly.

Moving closer, Jimmy saw that Groan was crouched beside some sort of mural.

'So much trouble,' Groan boomed, his forehead creased with the effort of thought. 'An' it all started wiv this fing.'

'No!' Jimmy cried. 'Don't touch that!'

The great barbarian reached into the mural and gripped its centrepiece: a golden-headed hammer. Then he yanked it out.

A stream of light illuminated the room.

It began as a moan – a long, low moan that developed into a roar and slowly became a deep and resonant scream. As Gordo looked on, a tiny pinpoint of light appeared under the bodies of the two grounded beasts. The pinpoint was joined by several others that widened as shafts of brilliant white light erupted all over the black giant and the dragon writhing around beside it.

Vanquish cried out, not just from his invisible mouth, but from the depth of his soul. Struggling under the force of the dragon's determined attack, he fought madly to escape the sudden, inevitable pull of the dimensional prison that opened up beneath it – a matrix gate that appeared from nowhere to form a net in the crater from which it had risen. A burst of energy enlarged the net, encasing both Moltenoak and his master in the breadth of its cast.

**How can this be** . . . ? Vanquish cried, as his cursed soul fell with him. **How can this** *beeeeeeeeeeee* . . .

*A mystery to me also,* Moltenoak boomed, his thoughts searing into the dark god's mind like fiery arrows. *But I'll go with you this time. This time, I'll make sure you never escape again . . .*

*Argghhhhhh . . .*

There was one final flash of light. Then the beast dissolved into a network of light, taking the great dragon with it . . . and a lengthy silence settled over the plain.

Gordo Goldeaxe stood on a nearby hillside, rubbing his head. It felt like he'd just woken up from a terrible dream – and now he just wanted to see his friend again . . . see him and ask him what the hell he thought he was playing at by trying to kill him! And speaking of mindlessly violent idiots, where in the seven hells had Gape got to?

Three horsemen rode past, their faces awash with glee.

'The soul-caskets are destroyed!' one cried. 'The soul-caskets have been destroyed!' Seeing Gordo, the group suddenly reined in their charges. 'Hey,' said one, sternly. 'Aren't you . . . the dragon-rider?'

'Me?' The dwarf sniggered at the suggestion. 'I doubt it: I hate heights. My name's Gordo Goldeaxe – I'm a mercenary.'

The soldiers shared a glance, then shrugged and resumed their gormless smiles. 'Ha! We destroyed the soul-caskets! The mindless folk of Dullitch are free once more!'

Gordo nodded at them. 'Good on you,' he said, masking his confusion with a friendly smile. 'You haven't seen a battleaxe by any chance, have you?'

But the group had already moved off.

Gordo sighed, and waddled back towards the

battlefield. En route, he passed a lone warrior, standing beside a horse. The man looked more like a ploughman than a soldier.

'All right,' said Gordo, conversationally.

The man turned to him and smiled, his eyes brimming with tears.

'I'm me again!' he exclaimed. 'I'm me!'

Gordo tried to put two and two together.

'Anything to do with a soul-casket?' he hazarded.

The ploughman put his head on one side and regarded Gordo.

'Are you a dwarf?' he asked.

Gordo nodded. 'Yeah,' he muttered. 'And you're a perceptive sort, aren't you? Hmm . . . you're, er, you're not from Dullitch, by any chance?'

The man beamed. 'Yes, yes I am!'

'Going back there?'

'Oh yes – this instant!'

'Care to give me a ride?'

The man nodded emphatically.

'Today,' he said, with relief. 'Today I'd give you the shirt off me back.'

Gordo chuckled under his breath.

'Just the lift'll do,' he said.


The light in the throne room died away.

'Well, I dunno,' Groan sniffed. '*That* din't seem ta do much.'

The big barbarian stepped away from the wall.

'Fink I'll break this 'ammer up,' he muttered. 'S'bin nuffin' but hassle eva since we found it in 'at ol' cave.' He looked up at the assembled group, and nodded at Diek.

'Fanks for carryin' me box,' he boomed, then turned to Burnie. 'An' farks for 'oldin' on to it. I'd prob'ly 'ave ended up in Trod uvverwise.'

His eyes moved from the group to the relieved face of Jimmy Quickstint.

'What you lookin' so pleased 'bout?' he said.

Jimmy smiled weakly . . . and tried very hard not to faint.

Behind him, Effigy, Diek, Burnie and Obegarde began to laugh. They continued to do so for a very long time.

# Epilogue

And for a time, Illmoor enjoyed a fragile peace. The throne of Dullitch was declared permanently vacant, much to the delight of the remaining citizens. The lords of Legrash, Spittle, Sneeze and Phlegm returned to govern their own kingdoms with the same mutual resentment that most of them had harboured for years.

Diek Wustapha went home to his parents – who were so shocked to see him that his father spent several months visiting the apothecary and his mother reverted to her old habit of talking in rhyme. The villagers of Little Irkesome forever referred to him as 'the boy that went bad', but he didn't mind that: it was just so good to be home.

Obegarde and Jimmy Quickstint remained in Dullitch, where they were quickly appointed to the city council. Burnie promptly stepped down from his position as council-chairman, advising the group to take Effigy Spatula as his replacement. Effigy himself wasted no time in accepting the position, and became the first and most popular Prime Minister in the history of Dullitch.

Groan Teethgrit and Gordo Goldeaxe tried to settle down to a life without adventure, but were soon lured to the heathen land of Trod in order to deal with a crisis that no one in Illmoor could ever have predicted . . .

## THE END

# Thanks to:

I would like to thank my editors at Hodder for their dedication to Illmoor, especially Anne McNeil (who fought my corner long before the deals were signed and who tirelessly edited Illmoors 2–6) and Venetia Gosling (who commissioned the series and baby-stepped me through the editorial stages of Illmoor 1). I'd also like to mention Joanna Moult and Naomi Pottesman, who have both slaved on my behalf over the small stuff. Last but not least, I again give thanks to mum, Barbara Ann Stone, for constantly picking me up when I was down . . . and always believing I had an important story to tell . . . even when I was ten years old.

# THE illmoor CHRONICLES

## The Ratastrophe Catastrophe

Illmoor, a country of contradiction, conflict and chicanery. A country riddled with magic, both light and dark ... and a capital city overrun with ... RATS.

The nice young man Duke Modeset hired to rid the city of its plague has run off with its children, and unless the Duke can track him down and bring the children back, he's DEAD ...

## The Yowler Foul-up

A terrible sect has arisen in Illmoor. They're dark, they're deadly and they're even more hellbent on the destruction of the city than the citizens themselves. All that stand between total chaos and the return of the dark gods are Duke Modeset (who doesn't like the place anyway), Jareth Obegarde (a vampire on his mother's side) and Jimmy Quickstint (who is about to do the wrong favour for the wrong man).

A thrilling story of darkness and destiny, where the brave step forward ... and fall over.

# The Shadewell Shenanigans

Groan Teethgrit and Gordo Goldeaxe have looted one village too many, and now the Lords of Illmoor are baying for their blood. Can Duke Modeset, exiled Lord of Dullitch, devise a plan clever enough to topple the duo AND Groan's equally reckless half-brother? Of course he can't, he's next to useless himself …

… but he does have one secret weapon: an extremely beautiful princess who seems willing to do absolutely nothing for the good of her country.

# The Dwellings Debacle

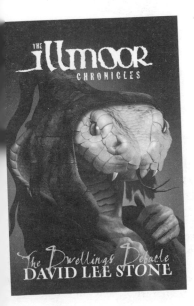

A dark enemy is about to make its presence felt in Dullitch … something even more twisted and evil than the citizens themselves.

But for Enoch Dwellings, famed investigator, it's a golden opportunity to shine. Unfortunately, the vampire detective next door has the same idea, and he never bites off more than he can chew.

There may be trouble ahead …

# The Vanquish Vendetta

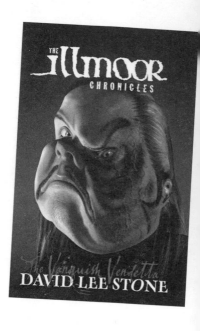

An evil impostor sits on the Dullitch throne, posing as Viscount Curfew. With bodies dropping left and right, suspicions are aroused. But it's nothing the Royal Society of Lantern Collectors can't handle ...

Meanwhile, King Groan Teethgrit is broke. A plan to flog an ancient hammer leads him, his brother and Gordo Goldeaxe back to Dullitch, where once again, they help make a bad situation so much worse.

# The Coldstone Conflict

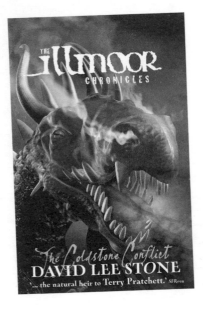

The evil Vanquish has returned to Illmoor and none can stand against him. To make matters worse, Illmoor's greatest hero is now a walking, talking, killing vessel of darkness.

Hope is fading fast ...

And yet there is one – ancient and powerful enough to challenge the dark god – who might step up to the task. Unfortunately, he's only interested in staying forgotten.

Can Illmoor unite to face its greatest enemy yet?

**www.illmoorchronicles.com**